ton...

ISBN 9781800941267

ISBN 9781800942400

Paperback and Amazon Kindle eBook editions

Published by Michael Terence Publishing

I Could Murder a Pint

Geoff Lambton

First published in paperback by
Michael Terence Publishing in 2024
www.mtp.agency

ISBN 9781800948839

Michael Terence
Publishing

Prologue

Fifteen Years Later

'Twice as many people are killed by vending machines every year than are killed by sharks.'

'Oh no, not that rubbish again.'

Jack Barnard flicked a switch on the steering wheel and Radio Z appeared on the display. His dad, sitting in the passenger seat wasn't best pleased.

'Hey! I wanted to hear the rest of that.'

'What for? We've heard it so many times it's just getting boring now.'

'That's not the point. The polite thing to do would have been to ask if anyone was listening to it and would they mind if you changed to another station. Didn't I bring you up to be good mannered?'

'No. You brought me up to be a grumpy bastard. Just like you. A chip off the old block and all that. Anyway, I'm only following your rules. You're the one who decided it is the choice of whoever is doing the driving that gets to decide what station we have on the radio, or what music we listen to.'

'Then maybe I should drive. It is my car after all.'

'Well buy me a car of my own then.'

'Do you think I'm made of money? Get yourself a job and buy your own car.'

'Yes. I do. Or do you consider being down to your last million makes you poverty stricken?'

'The last million won't last very long the way your mum is spending it on new shoes.'

'She always said you were a skinflint.'

'And you've always been a mummy's boy. When you were a kid you used to go running to her telling tales about everything I said and did. Mummy, mummy. Daddy said a rude word. Mummy, mummy. Daddy just squirted the cat with the hosepipe. Mummy, mummy. I just saw daddy have a pee in the garden on your roses. I couldn't do anything without you grassing me up. I bet you still do it.'

Another voice interrupted the conversation. It was Louis, spawled across the back seat.

'Will you two give it a rest? Some of us are trying to get some sleep.'

Barney was getting very irritated now. Louis was the son of his friend Liam. He was another chip off the old block. Not the sharpest tool in the box. And always wanting to sleep or eat. In fact, he was getting rather hungry now.

'If you must insist on keeping me awake, can we stop at the next services? I'm starving.'

The one thing they all agreed on was that they were all hungry and wanted to stop somewhere. But they couldn't agree on the location. Jack wanted to stop at the next services because it had a McDonalds. Barney wanted to go to the one after that as it had a KFC. Louis didn't mind. He would eat anything. Eventually Barney gave in, mainly because he needed the toilet urgently, and wasn't going to suffer any longer than necessary just to win the argument. So when they reached the next services, they pulled into the car park.

They were travelling from their home in the lake district, and their destination was Sunderland. They were going to the Stadium of Light to watch the FA Cup match between Sunderland and Slough Town. It was a game Barney particularly didn't want to miss. He had grown up around the Slough area but was firmly in the Sunderland camp today. He had been a Sunderland supporter since he was a little boy. He used to watch the football scores with his dad on Grandstand in the days when all the football matches were played at three o'clock on a Saturday afternoon before Sky TV took control and moved the date and time of games to suit themselves without any consideration of how it difficult it made things for travelling fans. He thought they were saying Thunderland and it was the coolest name of all the teams, then was hooked and could never wriggle free. Jack had eventually become a Sunderland supporter, having showed no interest in football until he was 10 years old. At the age of 20 he was now quite the fanatic. Louis wasn't quite so dedicated, but his dad hated football and was only interested in formula one and karate, so he decided to tag along with Jack to the football.

As they approached the various fast-food outlets, Barney spotted a pair of Cafeblam 73s, a coffee machine that was a new model back in the days when he worked as a vending machine engineer for a company called Vendetta. A company that Louis and his mum both worked for. But that was over 20 years ago. He assumed that the Cafeblam 73 would be obsolete by now. It wasn't the most reliable of machines. In fact one of them had an out of order notice on the front of it. The display was flashing Error Code 26. He couldn't resist. He spoke to the young girl behind the counter who looked stressed and was struggling to supply drinks quickly enough due to 50% of her machines being out of use.

'Excuse me. I used to repair those sorts of machines. That fault is very easy to fix. You just press a couple of buttons, then turn it off and back on. It should then work. I would be happy to get it working for you. It will only take a few minutes. I don't want paying or anything. Maybe just a free cup of coffee.

'Thanks, but there's no need. The engineer has just turned up. He's just gone to the gents. He should be back in a minute.'

The engineer arrived just as she was speaking. Barney was surprised at how young he looked. He was wearing an awful bright blue polo shirt with the company logo Flamingo Bleu proudly displayed. Vendetta had changed their name to Flamingo Bleu four years ago. Nobody was sure why. Barney introduced himself. The young lad wasn't exactly pleased about it.

'Alright mate? I used to work for you lot. Many years ago. I've fixed a few of these back in the day.'

The engineer wasn't impressed.

'Yeah. Great.'

'You're lucky. That's a nice easy one to solve.'

He looked at Barney as if he was something nasty he had to wipe off his shoe.

'I know. I don't need you to tell me how to do my job.'

'I wasn't. I was just being polite. Something you appear to have difficulty doing. OK, I'll leave you to it.'

He walked away, grumbling, and wishing he hadn't bothered talking to the ungrateful little sod. Jack and Louis bought burgers from McDonalds. Louis also added an extra-large portion of chicken nuggets to his order, as he often did. Barney fancied one himself, but after arguing against stopping at the service station with the McDonalds, he wasn't going to give them the pleasure of gloating if he had too one, so he settled for a sandwich and crisps from the M&S. While walking back to the seating area, he noticed that the Flamingo Bleu engineer still hadn't got the machine working and was frantically fiddling with his phone. Interesting. Barney deliberately chose a table where he could keep an eye on things.

Jack said, 'What do you think of our chances of winning the match today?'

Nobody answered him. Louis was too busy eating and playing a game on his phone. Barney was distracted. He was enjoying watching the engineer who was clearly struggling. There was no shame in that. It's not possible to remember all of the fault codes on all of the different machines. There was a good chance he hadn't come across a Cafeblam 73 before. There can't be too many of them still around. Way back when Barney was working, he would have gone to the car and looked it up in one of the many paper manuals he kept. But these days the manuals were all stored on a phone or could be found on the internet. But that didn't appear to be working for the young engineer on this occasion. Maybe he couldn't get a connection to his network. It looked like he was now trying to call someone for advice. But the lack of a connection was thwarting him. Barney was delighted.

'Oh dear, how sad, never mind.'

'What are you on about now Dad? I was asking what you thought of our chances of winning today were?'

'That lad was too proud to accept my help fixing the coffee machine. Now he's stuck. All he needs to do is press the reset button on the boiler overtemperature switch and turn the power off and back on. Serves him right. Miserable git. Sorry, what were you saying?'

'I was trying to talk to you about the match. Forget it.'

'I think we'll get beat. Come on. Let's get moving. I'll just have another quick visit to the gents, and we'll be off.'

Jack was getting rather pissed off with his dad, which wasn't unusual. Barney regularly pissed people off and was quite happy to do so. Jack, despite his earlier comment about being a chip off the old block was nothing like him. In reality, he was much more influenced by his mum Alison. Barney's accusation that he was a mummy's boy was an accurate assessment. It was hardly surprising. Alison had given up all hope of having any children due to the miserable years of her failed first marriage and the fact that she wasn't getting any younger. But then she unexpectedly became pregnant, and it was the greatest thing that ever happened to her. As a result, she completely spoiled him, often at the expense of Barney, and he loved it. He now was about to take an opportunity to get one over on his dad.

'Hey Louis. You know all about coffee machines, don't you?'

It was a fair assumption. Mary had got Louis a job at Flamingo Bleu as a vending machine operator. But it was also an over optimistic assumption.

'Yes. I know all about them.'

'How would you get that machine working?'

'I don't know how to fix them. My job is to clean them and then refill them.'

'That's hardly what I'd call knowing all about them.'

'But I remember what your dad just said. Something about pressing a temperature reset button on the boiler.'

'Yes, you're right. Then I'm sure he said you have to switch the power off and back on again. Okay. I need to act fast.'

Jack hurried over to the engineer.

'Press the reset button on the boiler overtemperature switch then turn the power off and back on. I don't particularly want to help you. You come across as a bit of a prick. I'm only telling you, so my dad won't be smug for the rest of the day. And don't bother saying thanks, you ungrateful twat.'

He did what he was told, and Jack hurried back to his seat. Barney returned and was disappointed to see that the coffee machine appeared to be working. They went back to the car and continued their journey. Jack was determined to get the conversation back to the football.

'So you think we're going to get beat?'

'How did he manage to get that machine working?'

'Stop obsessing about the machine. He fixed it because I told him how to.'

Barney was fuming.

'Why the hell did you do that? He didn't deserve help. He was a horrible little brat.'

'I know he was. But you were being a pain. Also I felt sorry for the girl who was struggling to serve drinks with the machine out of order. If it's any consolation, I was appropriately rude to him. And I was hoping once you stopped obsessing about that knobhead, you could answer my question about why you thought we are going to get beat today.'

'Ok. I will.'

'It's too late. I'm not interested now.'

'Obviously, Slough start as favourites, but we've been in good form lately, so you never know. Now would you step on it. I told Neil I would meet him for a pint and a game of darts in the Cliff before the match.'

But Jack was no longer interested. Louis was sprawled across the back seat and was feeling tired, thanks to his jumbo portion of lunch.

'Do you mind keeping it down while I get some sleep?'

'Certainly. I'm not surprised you're feeling drowsy. You're just like your dad when it comes to eating. Two bacon sandwiches for breakfast and two burgers with fries with a side of chicken nuggets for lunch.'

'My dad always gave me good advice about eating.'

'Really? He advised you to eat lots of burgers and bacon?'

'Yes. He read somewhere that it hardened your arteries. Mine should be nice and firm by now.'

'Er… I think he, and you also might have misunderstood. You think hardened arteries are a good thing?'

'Yes. As I understand it. If they are hard, they are a lot less likely to get broken. I would assume.'

'Listen Louis. I have been friends with your dad for a long time and he's a good person who means well. But if I were you, I would be seeking my nutritional advice from somewhere else.'

Louis promptly fell asleep, and they continued the journey in silence. Jack was driving at the exact speed limit, much to the annoyance of Barney who knew he shouldn't really complain about it. But despite sticking to the speed limit, they made good time and arrived at the Cliff just before one o'clock. Neil arrived ten minutes later. Neil lived in Sunderland and worked as a private investigator, and they had been friends for many years. He had a very sarcastic sense of humour. That was why he and Barney got along so well. They were two of a kind. They usually met before football matches for a drink and a few games of darts. Today they managed to squeeze in four pints each and a decent amount of darts. Jack and Louis settled for two pints each and Louis was hungry again, so sampled one of the local delicacies, a giant stottie full of ham and pease pudding before they headed off to the stadium, filled with optimism as usual.

1

Present Day

The sun was just appearing on the horizon on the remote island in the Outer Hebrides and was beginning to illuminate the ancient monastery which stood on the cliffs overlooking the Atlantic Ocean. The wind was whistling around the towers and the waves crashed against the shore. The landscape was magnificent. The reflection of the early morning sun was sparkling on the sea. It would be impossible to capture its true beauty on a photograph or painting. You would have to be there in person in order to appreciate it properly. Having said that you wouldn't want to be out there in just a T-shirt and shorts. The temperature wasn't quite so attractive. The monastery itself was a remarkable sight. It had been built many centuries ago by a bunch of Christian missionaries and was still populated, mainly by their descendants, plus a few others who had chosen to show their dedication to God by giving themselves a hard life, or had chosen to go there in order to find peace with themselves. It was still standing firm despite centuries of being battered by the relentless rain and strong winds. The people who built it could certainly give a few lessons to the construction firms of today. And they did it without the machinery and technology available these days.

Inside the monastery it wasn't much warmer. They had a few log fires burning, but it wasn't easy to heat a building this large and draughty. Not that the residents cared. They weren't there for luxury. Their spartan lifestyle was a choice they had made.

The monks were sitting down in the refectory to have breakfast. The food wasn't of the greatest quality. It wasn't the sort of breakfast that was being consumed by the rest of Scotland. If what was on offer here was served up in the Wetherspoons in Glasgow there would be a full-scale riot. But again the residents weren't there for luxury. This was another part of the austere existence the monks had chosen to endure. The Abbot didn't join them for breakfast. He would be enjoying something slightly more appetising when he bothered to get out of bed. But this morning his lie in was disturbed by the loud sound of the knocker crashing against his huge wooden door. It was the Prior, the second in command at the monastery. He wasn't happy about it.

'Couldn't this have waited until later?'

'I am so sorry Father. I have something I urgently need to tell you. And I'm afraid you won't like it.'

'Alright my son. Say what you need to say.'

'I have some news from the mainland.'

'News? How did you come by this news?'

'When the boat was in yesterday delivering our supplies, I obtained a newspaper.'

'This is a serious breach of the rules. No newspapers, no internet, no telephones. No unnecessary contact with the outside world.'

'I know Father. I will be only too pleased to receive the punishment I deserve for my weakness and disobedience. But this news is too important to keep to myself.'

'And what is this news that is so important you had to break your vows for?'

The Prior handed a newspaper to the Abbot. It was a copy of the Sun, two days out of date. The Abbot looked at it and his mood suddenly improved.

'Isn't this the newspaper that has photographs of young females wearing no clothes?'

'I don't know father. I have only read the headlines. I haven't looked at any of the pictures. I swear.'

The Abbot turned to page three and had a peek at a nineteen-year-old topless girl and quickly closed it again.

'I'm going to have to confiscate this. Do you have any others?'

'Yes. I have been receiving them regularly with every delivery. Would you like me to burn them?'

The Abbot opened the newspaper again and took another peek at the picture on page three.

'Er… No. Bring them to me and I will deal with them.'

'I am so sorry for breaching your trust.'

'I am very disappointed with you. But God teaches us forgiveness. I will overlook your sin on this occasion. But don't let this happen again. Just carry out the appropriate self-chastisement and we will say no more about it.'

'Thank you Father.'

'Now are you going to tell me this big news?'

'It's there on the front page.'

The Abbot read the front page and continued reading the story on page five, having yet another sneaky glance at page three in the process. His expression was getting more anxious with every line he read and every photograph he saw. When he'd finished, he folded up the newspaper and looked sternly at the Prior.

'This is indeed a concerning piece of news. You did right to come to me. It is vitally important that the Brothers do not hear of this. It must be kept secret between just the two of us. Do you understand?'

'Yes Father.'

'Now you must leave me. I require a little time on my own.'

'Apologies once again Father. You clearly wish to continue with your morning prayers.'

'Er… yes. Of course. Morning prayers.'

2

The house was completely silent, as you would expect it to be at three o'clock in the morning. There were a few animal noises outside which is normal in the lake district, but Barney was oblivious to them. He was in a deep sleep. Probably having a weird dream. But he couldn't help hearing the blood curdling scream that woke him up. Alison had already switched her bedside lamp on and was in a terrible state. He knew that the appropriate response would be to comfort her, even though he felt more like thumping her. He put his arm across her.

'There, there. It's alright. You just had a nasty dream. It's all over now. Just relax and go back to sleep.'

'No, I didn't have a dream, you idiot. It was real. It was fucking real!'

'What was real? What are you talking about?'

'I felt a tickle on my leg. When I reached down to scratch it, I felt something in my hand. When I put the light on and there was a great big spider in my hand.'

'Are you sure it wasn't a dream?'

'Yes. Of course I'm sure. It's still there on my bedside table. It's still wriggling.'

'You woke me up with a scream just because of a spider?'

'You hypocrite. It wasn't all that long ago that you woke me up during the night with a scream of your own.'

'Yes, but I was clawed by the cat right on my willy and was

bleeding for hours. I doubt that the spider drew much blood.'

Alison now felt a bit silly and stayed quiet for a few minutes. Barney rolled over and tried to go back to sleep. But she wasn't finished.

'Would you get rid of it for me?'

'In this age of equality you still expect the man of the house to get rid of a spider?'

'Stop trying to be clever and just get rid of it.'

'Ok. I'll do it first thing in the morning.'

'No. Do it now. I won't be able to sleep knowing it was there. Especially as it's still wriggling.'

He knew he would never be allowed to get back to sleep until he did what she wanted, so he climbed out of bed.

'I need to go to the bathroom anyway, so I'll flush it down the toilet.'

'No, no. You can't do that.'

'Why can't I?'

'It's still alive. Being flushed down the toilet is not a nice way to die.'

'What do you suggest I do? Fly it to a clinic in Switzerland?'

'Just put it outside.'

'Right. I'll bury it in the garden and make a little headstone.'

'No. It isn't dead. Just put it outside.'

He picked the spider up and took it to the bathroom where he flushed it down the toilet. He opened and closed the bathroom window in a futile attempt to fool Alison into thinking he had put it outside. Then when he finished what he needed to do he returned to bed and attempted to get back to sleep. But it wasn't going to happen.

'You flushed it down the toilet, didn't you? I told you not to do that.'

'It was in a bad way after you had half squashed it. It would have been cruel to let it live. Consider it a mercy killing.'

Alison didn't answer. She had a careful look around to see if there were any of the spider's relatives hanging around, then when she was satisfied she switched the light off. But neither of them could sleep. Barney could tell she was feeling anxious after her ordeal. So he did what any decent husband would do in this situation. Make her feel worse.

'I read somewhere that humans swallow an average of seven spiders every year.'

'Someone must be having fourteen then, because I haven't eaten any.'

'No, I don't mean by choice. I'm not saying people sit in front of the telly munching away on a packet of spiders and a cup of tea. They crawl into your mouth while you're asleep and you swallow them without knowing.'

'Yeuk! You'd better be winding me up.'

'No. It's true.'

Alison went quiet for ten minutes. Barney was almost asleep. But then Alison switched her light back on. She picked up her phone from the bedside table and googled 'Is it true that humans accidentally swallow spiders in their sleep?' She read the response, then she gleefully shoved the phone in his face.

'Look. It's not true. It says it's just an urban myth. It doesn't really happen.'

'That's great news. Do you mind if we go back to sleep now? I've got a busy day ahead tomorrow.'

'Busy? Doing what? Lifting a few heavy cans of beer? Watching some exhausting sport on television?'

'It's my turn to take Jack to school. There's nothing more exhausting than that.'

'I don't find it exhausting. I enjoy taking him.'

'That's because he is a little angel when his mummy takes him. He's a little devil when I take him.'

'Maybe it's the way you treat him.'

'Or maybe it's the way you treat him. You let him get away with anything. And if you find it such a pleasure, why don't you take him?'

'Because I need to go to the shops. Just get on with it and stop moaning. And if you bump into any of the teachers, try not to be rude to them. Or the other parents.'

3

Alison had been correct in her prediction of Barney's activities for the day. He was participating in his favourite hobby. Lying on the sofa watching sport with a quartet of lagers for company plus a packet of pork scratchings and two strawberry trifles. The sport on this occasion was snooker. Because it was midweek, there was no football, and he couldn't find any cricket that he was interested in. That left a choice of golf or snooker. He opted for the snooker, although there was a good chance he would fall asleep before the end. He enjoyed having the house to himself. Jack was at school, and the dropping off went reasonably peacefully. He didn't see any of the teachers and he successfully managed to avoid having to talk to the other parents at the school gates. He assumed Alison had gone shopping, probably for more new shoes. He wasn't expecting her back any time soon. The only other living creatures around were an annoying loud bluebottle and the two cats. George was a lot more tolerant of Barney these days. He was asleep on Barney's legs. Barney didn't discourage this. There was a house rule that if one of the cats was asleep on you, you weren't allowed to move. This was Alisons rule, not his. But it was a useful excuse to get out of doing a chore. Mildred was asleep on a different chair. Not too far away but not too close either. They had an uneasy truce. He still remembered the pain from the brutal unprovoked assault on his willy while he was asleep in his bed. While she couldn't forget his spiteful act of revenge by setting off a party popper next to her ears while she was asleep. She was still suffering from post traumatic stress disorder.

Barney's peace was not going to last for much longer. But it was the cats who were disturbed first. They both sat up simultaneously and their heads were looking frantically around. Then he heard the front door open and could hear an energetic panting. Perhaps Alison had been jogging. She occasionally went jogging, but this panting did not sound human. Then he heard her voice.

'Good boy. Sit. Sit. Good dog. Down boy. Down. Bad dog.'

The cats panicked and scurried behind the sofa. Barney was horrified. It sounded as if Alison had got a dog. She knew he didn't like dogs and had promised not to get one until Barney was dead. He got to his feet as she walked through the door accompanied by what looked like a jack russell.

'What the hell is that? You've got a dog without telling me? You know I don't get on with dogs. What's it doing here?'

'He's not an it. He's a he. Would you kindly not address him as it?'

'What is it… Oh I'm so sorry, what is his majesty doing here?'

'This is Arthur. Isn't he lovely?'

'No. It, he, whatever, isn't lovely. He's a dog. I don't find dogs lovely in any way whatsoever. But you're evading the question. Why have you got a dog? You promised me you wouldn't get one until I was dead.'

'Keep your hair on. It's only temporary. Douggie and Hazel are going to the United Arab Emirates for two weeks. They didn't want to leave him in a kennel for all that time so I said I would look after him. I assumed you wouldn't mind.'

'That's a mighty big assumption. And a false one. I do mind.'

'Oh well. It's too late now. You'd better get used to it.'

'What about the cats? They were terrified. Now they're trembling with fear behind the sofa.'

'I've heard it all now. You must be desperate if you think you can fool me with fake worry about the feelings of the cats. You've never shown any concern for them before.'

'Fake or otherwise, it's still a valid point. You might not give a hoot about my feelings, but you're going to upset your precious cats.'

'Oh they'll get used to it. So will you. You could even have a try at taking him for a walk if you wanted too. Who knows. You might even become friends with him.'

'It.'

Barney trudged back to his snooker, beer, pork scratchings, and strawberry trifles. He took a huge swig of lager and ate a trifle for comfort. The cats were still cowering behind the sofa. Then he almost jumped out of his skin when Arthur started licking his bare toes. He considered if it might be a good idea to go away for a couple of days. Or even weeks. He could pop down to Maidenhead to visit his dad. Or is that rather an overreaction? Is that just a case of out of the frying pan into the fire? Then Arthur knocked over his can of beer. That settled it. He was going to Maidenhead.

4

Two days later Barney arrived at his dad's house in Maidenhead. This was the house he had grown up in as a teenager. It was a modest terraced house with two bedrooms in a one-way street, from where you could walk into the town centre in twenty minutes. He had briefly moved out while he was living it up as a student in London, but then moved back in when he had finished university because he couldn't afford a place of his own. When he did finally move out to his own place, his mum soon followed. His parents had a fairly amicable divorce, and his mum moved to the lake district where she bought and ran a bed and breakfast. Barney loved it up there and would visit whenever he got the chance. It was a free, or at least very cheap holiday. Once he had retired, he moved there with his new wife Alison. They were near enough to her house to visit, or more importantly when they needed a babysitter, but were far enough away that he wouldn't have to pop round every five minutes to change a lightbulb or fix a drippy tap.

His dad, Cecil Barnard Senior was a cynical sort. Not quite as cynical as his son, but cynical enough to know Barney wouldn't visit without a good reason. It wasn't as though he never visited. They got on reasonably well, mainly because of their joint love of cricket, and they often attended England test matches in London together.

'Ok. What is it this time?'

'I don't know what you're on about.'

'What is your reason for coming here?'

'To visit you.'

'Yeah, right. How long have I known you?'

'All of my life.'

'Then we both know that you are bullshitting. You don't just visit. You only come here when you've got a hidden agenda. You either want somewhere to stay while you go to watch cricket or Sunderland or a rock concert, or Jack is driving you around the bend. Or Alison is driving you around the bend.'

'I'm offended. Can't a son just visit his dad without an ulterior motive?'

'No. Not in your case.'

'Okay. If you must know, I'm avoiding a dog.'

'That's better. I'll put the kettle on.'

His dad went into the kitchen to make tea. Barney followed him in.

'How's Alison? Does she not mind you leaving her on her own?'

'She's not on her own. She's got a son, two cats, the occasional spider, and now a dog for company. In any case why would she mind?'

'I don't know. I was just asking.'

'She's fine. She'll be glad that I'm out of the house for a while.'

'And what about my little grandson?'

'He's not so little now. He's ok. A bit of a pain in the neck at times and gets into trouble at school now and again. But in Alison's eyes he can do no wrong. But then he knows that and uses it against me. He's very crafty for a six-year-old.'

'What are you planning on doing while you're here? I'm sure you don't want to sit around here for two weeks talking to me.'

'I thought I'd go to Legoland, in Windsor.'

'Really?'

'No. Of course not. That's the last place I'd want to go. I used to go there to fix their coffee machines. It was full of spoilt brats and moaning parents. I hated going there.'

'What are you going to do then?'

'I'll pop out to some of my favourite old pubs. I'm not staying for two weeks. Just a couple of days. Then I'm going to Winchester. I might as well visit Mary and Liam while I'm down south. I won't get away with being away from home for two weeks. I'll have to go and face the dog at some stage. Also, we're due to go to mums for dinner on Sunday.'

'Yes, you wouldn't want to miss that. How is the old fruitcake? Still God's best mate?'

'I'm afraid so. She will have been to church on Sunday morning, so we can expect a detailed account of the vicar's sermon. I will try to say nothing but will be unable to resist and she will accuse me of blasphemy. It always happens that way.'

Cecil senior laughed. He still had some fond memories of Elizabeth but couldn't have remained married to her without being driven insane.

In the end he stayed for three nights. It wasn't too bad. He had a few relaxing pints in some of the pubs he used to drink in years ago. In one of the pubs, he saw a familiar face. It was a man called Steve Fletcher. A man who had once pointed a gun at him. He had last seen him being wheeled away on a stretcher into an ambulance after being slammed to the floor by Liam. He wasn't sure whether Fletcher remembered who he was, but he clearly recognised him from somewhere because they were looking across at each other. When Fletcher got up and walked to the bar he looked unsteady on his feet. Maybe he had consumed a few too many, or maybe he was still suffering from the karate throw from Liam. Or perhaps he had spent a couple of years in prison which had knocked the stuffing out of him. For a moment he contemplated walking over and talking to him and finding out what he'd been up to, but then thought better of it. Instead he finished his pint and walked out of the pub without looking back.

He was taking it easy with the beer. He anticipated that he might be in for some heavier sessions when he got together with Liam and Mary. Visiting them was really just a feeble excuse to get away. He would be seeing them in the next two weeks. They were all going on holiday together to Egypt.

The drive to Winchester only took a little over an hour. On the way he listened to the radio and was pleased when a quiz came on. There were five questions and he knew the answers to the first four. But the fifth one had him stumped.

'If two is company and three is a crowd, what are four and five?'

The first four questions were general knowledge, but this one was a bit cryptic. Several people phoned in and attempted to answer it, but nobody could get it right. By the time he arrived in Winchester he still didn't know the answer.

Later that evening, it was just Liam that came to the pub. Mary stayed at home. Their son Louis was only five years old, and their usual babysitter wasn't available. That suited Barney. He and Liam had a lot to catch up on. Liam had a lot to say about his job at the leisure centre. Mainly about the girls he worked with, and his boss who was about fifteen years older than him but was really hot and fancied him. Or so he imagined. Then they talked about Barney's situation.

'Do you really dislike dogs so much that you had to travel 600 miles to get away from it?'

'You're not allowed to call him it.'

'What are you supposed to call it?'

'He.'

'I never knew it was a he until you mentioned it.'

'I note your geography is up to the usual standard. It's only 287 miles from your house to mine.'

'Yeah, maybe. But it still doesn't explain why you don't like dogs. You should try to get to know him. Use him to your advantage. If you know what I mean?'

'No. I haven't got a clue what you mean.'

'Dogs can be very good for pulling.'

'What are you on about? He's a jack russell not a husky. And I don't have a sledge.'

'And you say I'm the stupid one. I don't mean that sort of pulling. I'm talking about pulling pulling. Pulling women. Take a cute looking dog for a walk in the park and they'll be all over you. It's a great way to break the ice. I used to do it all the time. I'd volunteer to take my sister's dog for a walk. It led to quite a bit of action for me.'

'I can't see it working for me. Besides, in case you've forgotten, I'm a married man.'

'I know, but you don't have to go all the way. You can still enjoy being chatted up by some hot totty.'

Barney thanked him for the suggestion but was unlikely to put the theory to test. When they were both single and went out to nightclubs, Liam was the one who got the girls. Barney usually ended up going home on his own. Or ended up with whichever one was left after Liam had taken the good looking one. So he doubted having a dog with him would make a great deal of difference.

They had a good drink as expected and wobbled their way back to Liam's house. Mary was still awake. Liam gave her a peck on the cheek, then Barney gave her a sloppy beery kiss on the lips.

'Hello my favourite ex work colleague. How I've missed you.'

Liam faked annoyance.

'What about me? Am I not your favourite ex work colleague?'

Mary ignored that and continued.

'Hello dickhead. You're still full of shit I see.'

'And you're as delightful as ever. How's life at Vendetta?'

'A lot easier now that you aren't there.'

'Charming. And how's my old mate Richard Bowles?'

'He's still in charge. But only just. I think he's losing his marbles. I believe you are the chief cause of that. I think he'll be gone soon anyway. There's some kind of takeover in the pipeline.'

'That usually means redundancies. Do you think your job is safe?'

'I should think so. I'm the only one on the management side who knows what they're doing.'

'That usually means you'll be the first one out of the door. Who is doing the takeover?'

'Some Belgian or French company called Flamingo Bleu.'

'Never heard of them.'

'They've probably never heard of you either.'

The following evening all three of them went out for a few drinks.

'I'm glad you found a babysitter for tonight, Mary. It wouldn't have been the same without you.'

'Really? You know what they say. Two's company. Three's a crowd.'

'That reminds me of a question I heard on the radio yesterday and it's been driving me round the bend ever since.'

'What was the question?'

'If two is company and three is a crowd, what are four and five?'

Mary had a little think then shook her head. Liam steamed in.

'Nine.'

'Nine? How did you get that?'

'Four and five is nine. And you think I'm the stupid one.'

'But what about the first part of the question?'

'That's irreverent.'

'Irreverent? I think you mean irrelevant.'

'That's what I said.'

Barney was relieved that he finally knew the answer but wasn't so happy that he'd been fooled by a trick question and was even less happy that the dumbest person he knew had solved it in a matter of seconds.

They left the pub and had a meal at their favourite Chinese restaurant. Barney did his usual trick of taking all the leftover food home to have for breakfast the next day. Then he started to feel a bit guilty and decided that he ought to go back home in the morning and help Alison with Jack and the dog.

5

It wasn't a bad drive home. It was a Saturday, and the roads were quiet. He had left early to beat the traffic. It had got quite heavy on the M6 just north of Birmingham and he was too tightfisted to pay for the toll road which would have possibly saved him half an hour. He could easily afford it, thanks to a combination of his lottery win and his reluctance to spend it. But it was a matter of principle. Why should he pay extra to use a road? Isn't that what you pay tax for?

By now he was feeling sleepy, so he opened the window and turned the radio up. He wasn't really listening to it, but suddenly took notice when Sharm El Sheikh was mentioned. They were soon going there on holiday. The presenter was trying to give away a holiday there.

'Today we are giving away a fantastic all-inclusive holiday for two in Sharm El Sheikh in Egypt. All you have to do is answer a simple question. And we have our first caller on the line. What is your name?'

'Lucy.'

'And where are you calling from Lucy?'

'Sheffield.'

'Okay Lucy from Sheffield. To win this fantastic holiday just answer this question. In what continent is Egypt?'

'Is it Asia?'

'No, I'm afraid it isn't. You don't win the holiday. Goodbye. Next caller. What is your name?'

'Simon.'

'And where are you calling from Simon?'

'Portsmouth.'

'Okay Simon from Portsmouth. To win the holiday you just have to tell me what continent Egypt is in.'

'I also thought it was in Asia.'

'Well now that you know it isn't, do you want to try a different answer?'

'I'm sorry, I don't know.'

'Okay. Goodbye Simon. So now we come to our third caller. I never would have predicted that. What is your name?

'Olivia.'

'And where are you from Olivia?'

'London.'

'Right then Olivia from London. To win this fantastic prize, tell me which continent Egypt is in.'

'Is it Europe?'

'No, it isn't I'm afraid. Goodbye. I never thought we would get down to the fourth caller. But here we are. What's your name?'

'David.'

'And where are you from David?'

'Milton Keynes.'

'Well David from Milton Keynes. I bet you can't believe your luck. You can now win this fantastic all-inclusive holiday for two in Sharm El Sheikh. Just tell me the continent Egypt is in.'

'Is it the Arab continent?'

'Oh for fu… Goodbye.'

'Does nobody want to win this holiday? Who's next?'

'I am Stephanie from Bristol.'

'Just give me the answer Stephanie. Please.'

'Africa.'

'Hallelujah.'

Barney had been listening to it all and was getting more and more angry. He had a good shout at the radio throughout the whole farce.

'Where the hell do they get these people from? Why come on national radio just to show everybody how stupid you are? Why didn't that person who said they didn't know just guess one of the other continents? There was always a chance they'd be right even if they didn't know. And what the hell is the Arab continent? Morons!'

He was feeling desperately tired but was reluctant to stop again. He only had another fifteen miles to go and just wanted to get home, despite the dog that was waiting there for him. Then he saw a blue flashing light in his mirror, and he could see it was a police car. He pulled towards the edge of the road to allow more room for the vehicle to get past. But as it went past him it swerved across in front of him and pulled up sharply. Barney had to brake unnecessarily hard and wasn't best pleased about it. He was even less pleased when the policeman got out of the car and approached his door. Barney deliberately didn't open the window and waited until the policeman gestured him to do so by doing a winding motion as if turning a handle.

'Sergeant Price. What a pleasant surprise. Don't you know cars have electric windows these days. Or have police cars still got handles you have to wind?'

'This is not a social call. So don't start being a smartarse.'

'I wouldn't dream of it. But I hope you've got a good reason for driving like you're in Starsky and Hutch.'

'That remains to be seen. I've been following you for a while and you driving is erratic.'

'Clearly not as erratic as yours. Look, I've just driven the best part of 300 miles and am desperate to get home. So whatever this is can you just get on with it.'

'300 miles without a break?'

'No, not without a break. I stopped at two service stations. I can't go that far without a toilet break.'

'So you've had a few drinks then?'

'Yes, I'm completely shitfaced.'

'You're admitting it?'

'Give me strength. I haven't been drinking. Just do a breathalyser or something and we can get this farce over with. I would like to get home.'

'Don't tell me how to do my job. I'm going to let you off this time, but you will have to report to a police station with your driving licence and insurance.'

'Let me off! I haven't done anything wrong. I ought to report you for harassment. And what do you think my mum have to say about that?'

'You can't hide behind your mum anymore.'

'I don't need to. I never have. You've got nothing on me. What did you mean by that anyway?'

'Your mum and I are no longer friends.'

Sergeant Price eventually drove away and Barney headed for home. He wondered what could have occurred between Price and his mum to make them no longer friends. He should be able to find out tomorrow. They were due to go to dinner at her house. He will ask her.

He walked through the door and Alison welcomed him with a hug and kiss. Then the dog got all excited and started jumping up at him. He didn't like it when dogs did that but did his best not to kick up a fuss. The next few days would be easier for everyone if he made an effort to get on with Arthur.

'I'm going up to have a lie down for an hour. I'm knackered after that drive, and I've just had an unnecessary encounter with Sergeant Prick.'

'OK. I'll see you in three hours. If you're serious about making friends with Arthur, perhaps you can take him for a walk when you wake up.'

Barney thought back to the conversation he had with Liam.

'You know, I might just do that.'

He only slept for just over half an hour and then lay there for a bit longer. He was thinking about the things Liam had said. Should he put his theory to the test? Would there be any harm in doing so? It's not like he would take it to the extreme.

Would he? What if he encountered someone really gorgeous and couldn't resist the temptation? Deep down he knew it was highly unlikely. But he knew there was some truth in what Liam was saying. When he was out in public with Jack when he was a baby, he would get lots of attention, especially from women. But that was slightly different. Having a baby with you suggested you weren't single. He went downstairs and spoke to Alison.

'I've decided to try taking the dog for a walk. Like I said, it might make the next few days more bearable if we could get used to each other.'

Alison thought it was not like Barney to be saying something like this and wondered if he had another motive. But she let it go for now.

'OK. Take him to the common. There will be plenty of other dog walkers up there. But don't let him of the lead yet. He needs to get used to you first so that he will come back when you call him.'

'Stop making a fuss. How hard can it be to take a dog for a walk?'

Barney set off for the common which was half a mile from the house. He found it harder than he expected. Arthur was strong and was pulling hard on the lead. Then it got even harder when they arrived at the common and the presence of other dogs raised his excitement levels even more. There were quite a few people walking their dogs, and it wasn't long before first contact was made. He heard a female voice behind him.

'My, what a lovely dog. What's his name?'

Barney turned around quickly only to discover it wasn't a

woman at all. It was a man with an effeminate voice.

'Errm… Thanks. He's called Arthur.'

'Lovely. What a lovely name.'

'Thanks. What's yours called?'

'Trevor.'

'Lovely.'

Barney wanted to move on, but Trevor's owner kept talking, while Trevor and Arthur sniffed each other's bottoms. Then he came up with a suggestion.

'My house is just over there on the edge of the common. Would you like to come back for a coffee?'

'No! No thanks. I don't have time. I need to go somewhere.'

'Maybe another time then?'

'Er… ok. Maybe.'

Barney said goodbye and hurried away. He would have to avoid this part of the common in future. His first attempt at using a dog as an icebreaker hadn't ended in a way he anticipated. He certainly wouldn't be telling Liam what had happened.

6

'I'm not feeling all that well. I must have flu coming on. I think I should just stay at home. You and Jack can still go.'

'Do you seriously in your wildest dreams expect me to fall for that? There's nothing wrong with you. Now get moving or were going to be late.'

'Okay, okay. Stop treating me like a little kid.'

'Then stop behaving like one.'

'Have I got time for a cup of tea?'

'Yes, but while you're in the kitchen have a look at the floor. There's something wrong with it. Theres a patch where it seems to sink when you stand on it. It feels like it's going to collapse.'

'Yeah, I'll have a look. Perhaps there's some hidden treasure down there. Or even a dead body.'

'Just get it sorted. I don't want Jack falling through there.'

'Just Jack? Are you not concerned that I might fall through?'

Alison laughed.

'As long as you don't cause too much damage when you fall. Go on. Make your tea and get dressed. We don't want to be late. Your mum doesn't like people being late.'

'All the more reason to be late.'

They set off on the drive of just over twenty miles, most of it along a hilly, twisty road but with breathtaking views. Barney used to enjoy the journey, but now he was less able to relax and take in the beautiful views following an incident when someone drove into the back of his car along this stretch of road, resulting in an earlier encounter with Sergeant Price.

They arrived at the house only ten minutes later than the agreed time. Barney could see nothing wrong with that, but Elizabeth dropped a hint of disapproval into the conversation.

'I got back home from church fifteen minutes ago.'

'Yes, but you can walk from your church to here in only five minutes. I've had to drive twenty miles.'

Elizabeth didn't bother answering that. She had made her point and wasn't in the mood for a meaningless argument.

As usual Jack was the centre of attention. Elizabeth spoiled him as much as Alison did. Barney wondered why Alison didn't just let him stay at home. He was surplus to requirements, apart from being the driver. Alison and Elizabeth would have mind numbing small talk and Barney would stay tactfully quiet as long as he could. He cringed when Alison started the ball rolling.

'How was church this morning Elizabeth?'

This resulted in ten minutes of waffle about the vicar's sermon, and mindless gossip about various friends of hers. Plus, there were several references to God, which sparked Barney off.

'It sounds like you've had a bit too much of the holy wine.'

'It is not holy wine! It is communion wine.'

'Or to give it it's proper name… wine.'

'Don't be so disrespectful. It's communion wine.'

'Right. The vicar gets a couple of bottles of Yellow Tail Cabernet Sauvignon from Asda for a tenner, says a prayer at them, and they become the blood of Christ. Then everyone takes a sip while eating one of those flying saucers but without the sherbet filling, which is the body of Christ. Makes perfect sense when you put that way.'

Alison, as usual had to step in and change the subject before things escalated.

'I'm starving. What are we having for dinner? Do you need any help?'

'No thanks Alison. It's all done. I'll be ready to dish up in ten minutes. We're having roast pork.'

Barney was pleased to hear that. His mum, despite her wacky ways was an excellent cook and roast pork with crispy crackling was one of her specialities. They sat down at the table and Elizabeth said grace. Barney stayed quiet and let her get on with it. But he thought of all the things he didn't like about Christianity, saying grace before eating was the biggest act of selfishness and hypocrisy. He was eager to move the conversation on to something else. There was something he was eager to find out. He needed to know why she was now an enemy of Sergeant Prick. But Alison spoke first, and he would have to wait for his opportunity.

'We're going on holiday at the end of next week.'

'That's nice. Where are you going?'

'Egypt. Just for one week unfortunately. It's all you can do at half term. Sharm El Sheikh. We're trying an all-inclusive holiday for a change.'

'Are you taking Jack with you?'

Another open goal for Barney.

'No. We thought we'd leave him at home alone to feed the cats and have some hilarious adventures fighting with burglars.'

'Oh you're so funny aren't you? You went on a skiing holiday in France not that long ago and Jack stayed with me. So it wasn't such a daft question.'

Alison had to intervene once more.

'Yes, Jack is coming with us. Mary and Liam are coming with us and bringing their little boy Louis.'

They continued the conversation for a while. Then there was a pause and Barney took his chance.

'I bumped into your friend Sergeant Price yesterday.'

'Did you?'

'Yes. Sergeant Price. Your friend.'

'Why are you saying it like that? Have you got some point to make?'

'No. I was just wondering if everything was okay between you.'

'No. Everything isn't okay between us. And you obviously already know something. You're not the most subtle person in the world.'

'He just mentioned that you were no longer friends.'

'No. We aren't.'

There was a long pause. Elizabeth was reluctant to discuss it any further, but Barney wasn't going to let it go. He broke the silence.

'Well? Are you going to tell us what happened?'

'No. You'll just make fun of me.'

'I won't. I promise.'

'Okay then. He came here for dinner a couple of weeks ago. Then he had rather too much to drink and made advances on me. Can you believe this? He drank a whole bottle of wine.'

Barney tried desperately not to laugh.

'One bottle?'

'Yes. A whole bottle.'

'One whole bottle?'

'Yes. What's the matter with you? Could you drink a whole bottle of wine?'

'One whole bottle?'

'Give me strength. Yes. One whole bottle.'

'I could drink a bottle of wine standing on my head. In fact I probably have done.'

'Wouldn't you be drunk?'

'I should hope so, or I would be asking for my money back.'

Alison stayed quiet but wasn't going to be allowed to stay out of it.

'Alison. You wouldn't drink a whole bottle of wine, would you?'

'Well I err… There have been the odd time when err…'

'I don't think it's all that clever to drink a whole bottle of wine.'

'Get real Mum. I could manage to drink two bottles, but then I would be certainly rolling all over the place and talking a lot of embarrassing rubbish.'

'That's what happened with Sergeant Price. He suggested we take our relationship to the next stage. I told him I wasn't ready to start dating again yet.'

This time he couldn't contain his laughter.

'Not ready? It's been seventeen years since your divorce.'

'I knew you'd make fun of me.'

'I'm not making fun of you. I just think if you're not ready after seventeen years, when will you ever be?'

'Well that's all you're getting out of me. I don't want to talk about it any more.'

'Alright. I'll talk about something else. Did I mention we were going out on Friday night? Would it be okay for me to bring Jack over and collect him on Saturday morning?'

'Oh, so you act all nice to me when you're in need of a babysitter. Well maybe I can't do it this time.'

'Come on. You say that every time, and then you still look after him.'

'Not this time.'

'Okay. I'm sorry. I didn't mean to be rude to you. We would really appreciate it if you would help us out by looking after Jack.'

'What's it for this time?'

'It's a night out arranged by the parents at Jack's school. We thought we ought to try and get to know some of the other parents. Plus there's a raffle to raise money for some equipment for the school which might benefit Jack.'

'I'll think about it.'

Alison was getting rather fed up with her role as peacemaker. She yet again sensed it was time to jump in and change the subject.

'Our kitchen floor has a problem. It feels like it's going to cave in at any moment.'

Jack chipped in. He was very good at eavesdropping on his dad's conversations and then repeating them in the hope of getting Barney into trouble.

'Daddy said there's a dead body under the kitchen floor.'

7

As always happened, Elizabeth didn't carry out her threat to refuse to look after Jack. Barney was confident she wouldn't and drove him to her house on Friday afternoon while Alison stayed at home getting ready for their evening out. He had managed to get away from his mum's house without too much fuss and there was plenty of time to drive home and get changed into some going out gear. But he was about to have an unexpected delay. With five miles of his journey still to go, his phone blasted out the delicate tones of Action by Def Leppard. He tried to answer it, but for some reason his phone wasn't connecting to his hands free device. He was expecting some important phone calls, so he pulled his car over and parked next to a field in the middle of nowhere. Much to his annoyance it was a junk call from some clown who said he was in the area and would you like your carpets cleaned. He told the man in no uncertain terms where to shove his carpet cleaner. Then he took a deep breath and prepared to drive on. But just before he moved off, he spotted a sheep next to the fence. The sheep appeared to be struggling to get away from the fence. It looked like a barbed wire fence and the sheep was caught on it. He wasn't sure what to do. Animals were not his thing. But he couldn't leave it suffering.

After sitting there for a while trying to think who he might call, he decided to take action himself. He found a small gap in the fence and squeezed through it. Then he walked along the inside of the fence to where the sheep was stuck. He didn't really want to touch it but plucked up the nerve to grab it and pulled as hard as he dared. But the sheep would not budge. He tried several times without success. Just as he was on the verge of giving up, a police car pulled up behind his car. His initial reaction was one of relief. The police would surely help him, or at least know who to call. But his relief turned to frustration when Sergeant Price climbed out of the car.

'Not you again. Are you following me around. I might have to make a complaint of harassment.'

'I was just passing. And it is my duty to investigate when I think there's a crime being committed.'

'Well you're wasting your time. Again. There is no crime being committed here.'

'Do you think not? You're trespassing for a start. And stealing sheep is a very serious offence.'

'I'm not trying to steal it you dozy bastard. I'm trying to rescue it. It is caught on the barbed wire. Now that's offence. Get it? Ha ha. Never mind.'

'You are seriously pushing your luck. You are very close to being nicked.'

'Yeah, yeah. Meanwhile would you mind doing something useful like giving me a hand?'

'Stuck on the fence. A likely story. Sheep rustling is on the rise around here and we are stamping down on it.'

'And what exactly was I supposed to do with my stolen sheep? Squeeze it into my boot? Carry it single handed to wherever you would sell a stolen sheep? Come on. Use a bit of common sense. Just look at it. You can see it's stuck. Just help me free it.'

Price realised Barney was right and reluctantly decided to help.

He wriggled his way through the gap, but slipped on some mud in the process, and landed with a big messy splat. Barney tried hard not to laugh. Or perhaps he didn't try his hardest. Price could see him smirking, which did nothing to improve his mood, but he knew he didn't have much choice but to help. He worked his way over to the sheep and pulled out a penknife which he used to cut away some of the wool which was attached to the barbed wire. After that they didn't need to do anything else. Now that there was less resistance the sheep pulled itself free and ran off across the field in delight.

'Thank you Sergeant. You have been most kind and helpful. We make a good team. But I think perhaps you should have a word with the farmer. Is it even legal to keep sheep in a field with a barbed wire fence? I could see them getting stuck all day long. And it would be a waste of police resources if you spent all day rescuing sheep instead of catching criminals.'

Price stormed off without saying a word. He got back in his car and drove off, still covered in mud.

8

They didn't have any real friends among the other parents at the school. The school gates were a strange place socially. For a start it was mainly women collecting the children, either mothers, grandmothers or childminders, so Barney was already at a disadvantage when it came to making friends. They were mostly in their little cliques, and there were only two or three parents who politely smiled or had the occasional chat with Barney or Alison. Another obstacle was Jacks behaviour. If he had had a spot of bother with one of his classmates such as shoving them or swearing at them or shoving worms down their trousers, the parent of that child would retaliate by snubbing Barney or Alison and making sure it was clear who was to blame for their son's naughtiness.

Barney wasn't keen on going. He wasn't the sort who normally turned down the chance of a drink, but this didn't appeal to him. Alison had tried to convince him that it was a chance to get to know some of the other parents, and it was possible that they may be more friendly on a night out in the pub and being a bit pissed than they were at the school gates, although it could just as easily work the other way. Alcohol didn't always have the effect of causing people to be more friendly. But as he had explained to his mum, the money raised from the raffle could benefit Jack, so they felt it was the right thing to do to take part.

They took a taxi because they both fancied a few drinks. The evening started pretty much as they expected. Barney had a couple of pints and Alison was on the white wine. They were given a few polite hellos, but nobody stopped to have a conversation with them. Barney was quite happy with that, Alison not so much. There was a tremendous buffet provided, so they had some food and stopped worrying about whether anyone would talk to them.

Later in the evening it was time for the raffle. The organisers had done a marvellous job arranging prizes. They had visited local businesses asking for donations and they had ended up with some quality prizes that were well worth winning. The first prize was a spa day at a local hotel, and the second prize was a meal for two at a high-class restaurant called the Fisherman's Friend. Barney wanted to win that. He'd been there before and would happily do it again. Sadly, his ticket wasn't drawn out. The third prize was a flight in a glider, which had been donated by the gliding club at an airfield not too far from where they lived. He wasn't so bothered about winning that. But lo and behold, one of his numbers came out of the hat. He was happy to win something, even though he was unlikely to make use of it.

The rest of the evening passed harmlessly by. They had a lot more to drink and were enjoying themselves without caring that nobody was talking to them. Towards the end of the evening a man came up to him and introduced himself.

'Hello. I believe you are Jack Barnards dad.'

'Yes, I am.'

'I am Stuart, father of Stephanie Adams. She is in the same class as Jack.'

'Pleased to meet you.'

Stuart waffled on for a while about the school and their kids. Barney pretended not very convincingly to be interested. Then

Stuart moved the conversation around to suit his ulterior motive.

'We both had a stroke of luck in the raffle. I won the meal for two at the Fisherman's Friend.'

'Congratulations. I've been there before. It's very good.'

'Hmm. It sounds a bit like a cough lozenge to me. I'm not keen on fish anyway.'

'They don't just sell fish. They do all kinds of stuff. They do very good steaks. And…'

'Maybe so. But I'd have much rather have won the flight in the glider. I bet you're pleased about that.'

'No, not really. I'm not good with heights. Alison here might have to use it.'

Alison grinned politely and shook her head.

'I don't think I'll be doing it either.'

'Hey, I've just had a great idea. We should swap prizes. You two have the meal in the restaurant and I'll take the glider flight. Would that be okay with you?'

Barney was about to agree, but he paused before responding. Suddenly the conversation had taken on a different dynamic.

'No, it's not okay. I'll just keep the glider flight.'

'But you said you weren't keen on doing it.'

'You must have misheard. I'm very much looking forward to it.'

'You are contradicting yourself. I don't understand you.'

'No, but I'm beginning to understand you.'

Stuart walked away without bothering to say goodbye. Alison was puzzled. She asked him about it in the taxi home.

'What was that all about? You weren't very nice to him.'

'I thought I was reasonably restrained in the circumstances. I could have easily been a lot less nice to him. He came over and talked to us and made polite conversation, but all he really wanted was to swap prizes. He wasn't interested in us. Once I'd realised what he was up to, there was no way I was going to give him it. The selfish bastard.'

'But you won't even use it. We could have had that meal in the Fisherman's Friend.'

'Let's do that anyway. We can afford it.'

'What did you just say? There must be something wrong with my ears. I need to get them tested.'

'Very funny. And you never know. I might just do the glider flight after all.'

9

It was Monday morning, and Barney wanted an easy day after all the travelling of the past week. Alison had already taken Jack to school and was bustling around the house in a manner which made Barney suspect she was going out somewhere. Barney was sitting in the garden in his favourite chair in the shade under a cover on top of some wooden posts, in the place which afforded the best view of the nearby hills. He liked to sit here with a beer on a warm evening, especially if it was raining. He found the noise of the rain splashing onto the roof while he was cosy and dry was the most relaxing sound in the world.

Today it wasn't raining. There were a few clouds around, but the sun was peeping through sporadically. Nor did he have a beer. It was a little early in the day for that. Instead, he had a mug of tea and a bacon sandwich with a large dollop of ketchup. The dog was lying on the ground next to him half asleep. Arthur seemed to have taken a liking to Barney, and Barney thought Arthur wasn't too bad for a dog. But as was often the case, his attempt to have a nice relaxing day was cruelly thwarted. He had barely finished his tea and sandwich when Alison came out and disturbed him.

'Mrs Solly has been on the phone. She wants one of us to go to the school. She says she has something serious to discuss about Jack.'

'Not again! How many times is that this year?'

'Too many.'

'What is it this time? Did he fart in class or something?'

'She didn't say.'

'It's bound to be much ado about nothing. It usually is. Do you want to go?'

'No. I can't. I'm going out somewhere. It's about time you took your turn.'

Barney didn't ask where she was going. Nor did he argue about going to the school. He knew there was no way out of it. There was a nice pub near the school that sold superb chicken wings. He could pop in for a pint and snack once he'd got Mrs Solly out of the way.

He had no intention of hurrying there. He picked up his phone and played games for half an hour. Then he had a look at the messages on a WhatsApp group he was part of. It was a group of Vendetta employees who used the group to either slag off the company, complain about unreasonable customers they have had to deal with, ask each other for technical advice, or just generally take the piss out of each other. He had stayed in the group after he had left the company, mainly just so he could keep getting reminded how happy he was to not have to go to work again. There wasn't much activity on the group this morning. He assumed they were all hard at work. He smiled at the thought of it. Then he came back to reality and headed to the car.

Twenty minutes later he reported to the school reception and asked for Mrs Solly. She was the deputy head of the school and usually dealt with matters like this. Whatever this particular matter may be. She was a strict teacher who didn't smile much. A bit like the teachers back in the days when Barney was at school. She arrived at the reception and led him to her office where they sat down.

'Thanks for coming Mr Barnard.'

'That's alright. Is Jack OK?'

'Yes, he's fine. This morning, he was telling everyone that there's a dead body under your kitchen floor.'

Barney laughed.

'The little rascal.'

'Do you find it funny Mr Barnard?'

'Yes. I thought it was meant to be funny. Sorry.'

'I told Mrs Barnard on the telephone that this was a serious matter. I'd appreciate it if you take this seriously.'

'I will do. If you would care to tell me what he did.'

'I've already told you what he did.'

'Ah. You mean the dead body thing is the actual issue? I thought you were just making light-hearted conversation before getting on to the real problem.'

'No. This is the real problem. Saying these things can frighten some of the other children. One girl was in tears.'

'Oh do leave off. She won't suffer any permanent damage. He's only six years old. He barely knows what a dead body is.'

'I don't want this happening again.'

'Fair enough. When we dig up the floor next week you can send the girl around to the house and she can see there's no dead body. In fact, why not bring the whole class? Make it like a school trip.'

'Now you're just being silly.'

'You started it.'

'You will not speak to me like that.'

'Wait a minute. I'm not one of your six-year-olds.'

'Then stop acting like one.'

Barney was getting pissed off with Mrs Solly. He just wanted to get out of there. He decided that the quickest way to achieve that would be to say the things she wanted to hear.

'Right. What is it you would like me to do?'

'Talk to him. Explain to him what he said was inappropriate. And he shouldn't do it again.'

'I'll give it a try. But he doesn't usually listen to what I say.'

'Perhaps Mrs Barnard can do it?'

'That's the most sensible thing you've said since I got here.'

On that note they ended the meeting. Barney trudged out of the school gates back to his car, wondering how Mrs Solly would have coped with his classmates back in his schooldays. They came out with much worse stuff than Jack's comments.

He popped into the pub for a pint of lager and ten chicken wings with a barbecue dip. Once he'd finished his treat, he drove home. He explained it all to Alison and suggested she try talking to Jack. In general they were in agreement in their view of the way Jack was treated by the school. They had suspected for some time that he had some kind of what was referred to as 'special educational needs' such as autism or

ADHD, but the school didn't appear to be making any effort to get him assessed.

'Even if you think it was a huge overreaction by the school, that floor need sorting, dead body or no dead body. Can I leave it in your hands? Start making a few phone calls and get someone in to look at it.'

'Yes, alright.'

'Today?'

10

Alison would soon regret leaving the solution to the kitchen floor in Barney's hands, as was often the case in situations like this. It took four days to get someone come and look at it. Barney had been asking for recommendations on a local social media group and as always he went for what appeared to be the cheapest option. As a result, two men turned up and they didn't fill Alison with confidence. Her first impressions were that the older looking one who appeared to be in charge was an arrogant arsehole and his companion was a grinning imbecile. She wasn't in the mood to listen to the drivel they were spouting so she left them in the kitchen with Barney and went outside to do a bit of gardening. She returned to the kitchen half an hour later and nothing much appeared to have changed. She wasn't happy.

'Have you actually done anything in the time I've been gone? Or are we paying you to just stand around all day scratching your arses?'

They didn't respond directly to Alison, which did nothing to improve her opinion of them. Instead, they talked directly to Barney.

'She's a feisty woman your missus.'

'You'll find out exactly how feisty in a minute. I asked you a question. What have you been doing all of this time?'

'We've been conducting an investigation of the works required. I am about to explain it to your husband. I'll tell you what darling. How about you put the kettle on and make us a nice cup of tea? My gob is drier than a nun's…'

'If you talk to me like that again, the only thing your gob is going to get is my fist. Now tell me what you've found before I get really annoyed. Darling.'

'Yes errr… Well the first thing we need to do is take the flooring up and have a look underneath to see exactly why it has sunk.'

'Wow! There's no need to blind me with science. Tell me in words a woman could understand.'

Barney decided to intervene before someone got hurt. But he didn't have time to get his words out. Alison turned her anger on to him.

'Why did you hire this pair of bell ends? You're just like Basil Fawlty in that episode of Fawlty Towers where he hired that one-armed Irish builder because he was the cheapest.'

'I think you are getting your sitcoms mixed up. The Irish builder in Fawlty Towers had two arms. The actor who played him, David Kelly also played a waiter who only had one arm in Robin's Nest, which was a spin off from Man About the House. You know the one. You named the cats after the characters George and Mil…'

'Shut up! Just shut up! I don't want to hear another word out of you. Just get these cretins out of my house. I'll look for someone else to do it.'

'Yes, at once Sybil.'

Barney decided it would be a good idea to get out of the house for a while otherwise he was going to get an earbashing with Alison in this mood. Once he'd followed her instructions and got rid of the unwanted builders, he volunteered to take the dog for a walk. He would put Liam's theory to test again. It would be much more pleasant to chat with a friendly dog walker than be given a hard time at home.

He walked Arthur to the common again, but to a different part. He didn't want to bump into the man who fancied him. There were plenty of other people out with their dogs, but one in particular caught his eye. She was a classy looking lady, probably slightly older than him with a figure-hugging dress and a hat that made her look like she was on her way to ladies day at Royal Ascot. She was accompanied by a well-groomed poodle that looked like it had just had a shampoo and blow dry. Barney sneakily manoeuvred Arthur towards them. Then he decided he would speak first.

'Hello. My, what a lovely little dog. What's his name?'

'Her.'

'Oh, I'm ever so sorry. What's her name?'

At this point Arthur started slobbering and pulling hard on his lead, desperate to get to the poodle. The lady squealed.

'Oooh, oooh. Get that filthy beast away from me at once.'

'Sorry, I was only trying to be friendly. I just thought your poodle was nice.'

'Friendly? Why do you want to be friendly? Are you some sort of pervert? Get away from me before I call the police.'

Barney dragged Arthur away as quickly as he could. He was sure there were people around who must have heard her outburst. This would now be another part of the common he would have to avoid. If he didn't just give up the dog walking altogether. He wandered around for a little while longer. He got a smile from two women and a man, but his heart was no longer in it. He just wanted to get back home. The advice he got from Liam was rubbish. He was kicking himself for believing it in the first place.

11

Mary and Liam were relaxing in a pub garden in Winchester. Their son Louis was running around with two other kids. One was a five-year-old boy, the same age as Louis and the other was a six-year-old girl. It was an ideal place to go with kids. There was a fenced in garden which had swings, a slide, a roundabout, and various other things they could climb on. Louis would happily stay there for hours if they let him. They also served decent food, which was good for Liam in particular who was always hungry. It was within walking distance of their house, so they could have a few drinks without having to worry about driving. It also gave them a chance to talk.

They talked about work. Liam enjoyed working at the leisure centre. It didn't pay much, but it was a steady job. He had no worries about takeovers and redundancies. Mary on the other hand was worried. The takeover rumours were getting stronger every day. Liam wasn't the smartest of blokes and couldn't understand why Mary could be losing her job. He tried to sympathise with her when she tried to explain it all to him. What he did understand was that she earned a lot more money than him and they would struggle to make ends meet if the worst did happen. At least she would get a decent redundancy payment. She had been there for twelve years. He sometimes was envious of Barney's good fortune in winning all that money, but he didn't begrudge him it. And he had given them ten thousand pounds out of his two million winnings which came in very handy just at the time they moved in together and had a baby.

Liam just remembered something and thought he had better

ask about it.

'Weren't you supposed to do some kind of test today?'

'Yes. But I would hardly call it a test. It was all a complete waste of time if you ask me?'

'What was it all about?'

'It was an Online Safety Assessment. The powers that be at the company decided all employees had to take the assessment and pass it.'

'What does that mean?'

'Come on Liam. Even you can figure that one out. It's an assessment about online safety.'

'It could have been an assessment about safety carried out online.'

'No. It wasn't. It was an assessment about online safety.'

'So it really should have been called an Online Safety Assessment Online.'

'Whatever.'

'How did it go?'

'I watched a video for fifteen minutes and I didn't understand a word of it. Then I was asked two questions which I didn't understand either. It gave you a choice of three answers. I just guessed the middle one, like I do when I'm watching the Chase or Tipping Point. I got one of them right and the other one wrong.'

'So does that mean you failed?'

'No, I don't think so. A message came up at the end saying

congratulations, you have successfully completed the assessment.'

'Well done. I knew you could do it. And now you work for a company who have employees who are presumably safe online.'

'Yeah. Something like that.'

Their conversation about work was interrupted by the ringtone of Liam's phone.

Mary pretended that she was irritated.

'Who the hell is that, bothering us now?'

'It's only Barney.'

'What does that dickhead want?'

'I don't know. How about I answer and ask him?'

'I suppose so.'

Liam smiled at her and told her he knew she didn't mind really. He answered the phone. At first all Mary could hear was Liam saying 'Yes' at regular intervals. Then he started sniggering. This soon turned into full blown laughter. By the time he ended the call he was in hysterics. Mary imagined Barney fuming at the other end.

'What on earth was that all about?'

Liam couldn't get his words out. It took him a few moments to compose himself.

'When he was down here last week, I told him that taking a dog for a walk was a great way to get talking to women. He took my advice.'

'And why is that so hilarious?'

'His first attempt attracted a gay geezer who invited him back to his house. Then when he tried again, he encountered a woman who accused him of being a pervert and threatened to call the police.'

Mary joined in the laughter.

'I assume he was very calm and dignified about it?'

'Of course he was.'

'I bet.'

They both had a good laugh about it. Then Mary turned serious again.

'Where did you get the idea? I hope you've not been trying it too.'

'No. Of course I haven't. I've never taken a dog for a walk in my life. I told him my sister had a dog and I used to take it for walks. But it wasn't true. I just had a feeling if I suggested it to him, he would do something stupid. Looks like I was right.'

Mary started laughing again.

'Maybe we should go and visit them soon. I haven't seen Alison for a while. And Louis likes to see Jack.'

'We'll see them soon enough. We're going on holiday with them.'

'Yes. I'm really looking forward to that. We usually just manage a long weekend in Eastbourne. Apart from the flight. I'm scared of flying.'

'Tell me about it. I remember the only other time I flew with you. I shan't be sitting next to you. I'll arrange for you to sit next to Barney. I don't think he's all that keen on flying either.'

12

The Basil and Sybil antics continued at Barney Towers. Alison had taken over the search for someone to repair the damage on the kitchen floor and had put in considerably more effort than Barney had. Where he hadn't looked beyond who was the cheapest, she looked at companies who were in trade groups and had recommendations from satisfied customers. As a result, they had a visit from a builder who took only a few minutes to tell them exactly the same thing that the previous ones had wasted so much time to reveal. They would have to lift the floorboards and find out what is causing the problem. They had a slot tomorrow afternoon when they could do that. Alison told them to go ahead.

The next morning Alison had to go out again, so she reluctantly had to trust Barney to deal with the builders. She had half jokingly warned him not to do a Basil again and bring back the useless builders. But it was highly unlikely. Even he recognised how bad they were. So she was fairly optimistic when she returned home. That optimism quickly evaporated when she saw the look on his face. It was a look of shock and revulsion. He took her into a different room away from the kitchen.

'What's wrong? What has happened?'

'I don't know how to tell you this. You'd better sit down.'

'Just get on with it will you?'

'This is going to come as a shock. You know how I was joking about a dead body being down there?'

'Yes.'

'Well that's exactly what they did find.'

Alison stayed quiet for a few seconds. Then she gave an apprehensive laugh.

'Get out of it. You're having a laugh.'

'Do I look like I'm laughing? There were human remains down there. The police have been called. We might have to wait some time for our kitchen to be fixed.'

He eventually managed to convince her that it was true. He made her a mug of tea and they sat there not saying much. After she had finished her tea, she couldn't resist going into the kitchen. Barney tried to tell her she shouldn't go in as it was probably now a crime scene, but she wasn't going to be stopped. It was her house, and she had every right to take a look. As she wandered to the kitchen she was surprised to find the builders still there.

'Hello. I'm really sorry about this. It must have been a big shock for you.'

'No, not really. It's not that bad. Some water had leaked down there over the years and had rotted some of the timber. We will have to replace them, but we should be able to put it right in a couple of days. Three days at the most by the time the new floor dries.'

'Will the police allow you to keep working? I thought it was now a crime scene.'

'Sorry, you've completely lost me now.'

'I'm talking about the body.'

'Body? What do you mean? What body?'

'The body that… That bastard! I'm going to fucking kill him.'

'Are you alright love?'

'Just hang on a minute. There's going to be a dead body in here after all.'

She stormed into the room where Barney was laughing hysterically and flung the empty mug at him. He ducked in the nick of time, and it shattered loudly against the wall.

'You rotten git. What an awful trick to pull.'

'A bit like the trick you pulled on me in Cornwall. Now you know how it feels.'

Alison laughed. Not so much at the prank Barney had just played on her, but at the memory of how she with the help of the other members of the darts team had made such a fool out of him on their trip to Cornwall. She reluctantly accepted that it was a fair revenge. They both had a laugh and hugged. What they didn't realise was Jack was playing in a nearby room and had overheard most of their conversation.

The following morning Alison took Jack to school. Barney stayed at home but couldn't have his usual unhealthy fried breakfast because of the lack of a floor in the kitchen, which was going to be the case for another three days. They had set up a coffee and tea station in the lounge, but if he wanted a bacon sandwich he would have to go out and get one from somewhere else. He decided to wait for Alison to return home and see if she would like to go out for breakfast. He made a cup of tea and waited.

Alison arrived home and agreed it would be a good idea, but

she wanted a cup of coffee first. As she was drinking it her phone rang and much to her dismay it displayed School on the screen.

'What do they want now? He's only been there for forty-five minutes. He hasn't had time to upset anyone yet. Has he?'

'Answer it and we'll soon find out.'

Alison answered the call.

'Hello… Hello Mrs Solly… Yes… Yes… No… Okay. We will be there as soon as possible.'

The call ended abruptly.

'What's he done this time? Eaten the goldfish?'

'Telling more tales of dead bodies. You'd better get round there.'

'Why me? I went last time. It's your turn.'

'Because you are the one that put the idea in his head. And you are the one that took it a step too far with your stupid prank. You can sort it out.'

'What about breakfast?'

'Sort this out first, then I'll meet you in that pub near the school. We'll have brunch there.'

Barney liked that idea. A pint of lager and ten chicken wings would be a great breakfast. But he wasn't relishing another confrontation with the frosty faced Mrs Solly. He wasn't going to rush. He made another cup of tea.

He eventually made it to the familiar surrounds of Mrs Solly's office.

'Mr Barnard. This is starting to get out of hand. Did you even speak to Jack about his behaviour?'

'Yes, of course I did. We both did.'

'Well it doesn't appear to have worked.'

'Why? What has he done?'

'He is now saying some builders discovered the dead body and the police have been called.'

'Why can't you lighten up a bit? Is he really doing any harm?'

'I will not have you coming in here and tell me to lighten up a bit.'

'Isn't it healthy for a boy to have an imagination?'

'Mr Barnard. I will tell you for once and for all. You need to something about this.'

'What do you suggest? Therapy? Hypnotism? Lock him in a cupboard? We've tried talking to him. It's not working.'

'That's your issue. You are the parents. Sort it out.'

'That's just a cop out. The school has a responsibility too. One of the reasons we chose this school was because it boasted it was very good for children with special educational needs. But I'm not seeing it. We're still waiting for him to be assessed. How much longer do we need to wait? What are you doing about it?'

'Mr Barnard. There is a procedure we are required to follow. Meanwhile I have a duty to all the children at this school.'

Barney was by now getting the serious hump with this woman. He stood up and headed towards the door.

'Right. I've got an idea. I will deal with it. I promise you he won't mention any dead bodies from now on.'

He didn't really have an idea. Not any good ones at least. But he wanted to get out of there and go for some food. He met Alison in the pub and explained everything. She wasn't impressed. Barney got the feeling she was blaming him for their son's behaviour. But in truth what he needed was a proper diagnosis from an expert and then have some ammunition to use when the school, and other parents just looked upon him as a naughty boy.

13

It was Friday evening, and the builders were clearing away their equipment having finished the kitchen floor. Barney was toying with the idea of taking the dog for one last walk. Arthur would be returning home on Sunday when Douggie and Hazel returned from their holiday. He wanted to have at least one success story for Liam following the way he had laughed so much at him. But was it worth the risk? What if it went wrong again? There wouldn't be any area of the common left where he would dare go. After the disasters of his two previous attempts, he vowed never to do it again. At the same time, he didn't want to give Liam the pleasure of laughing at him again. And he even contemplated making up a story of an amazing encounter with a beautiful woman. Liam wasn't the most difficult person in the world to fool, and there was no chance of him finding out it was all made up. But then Alison came in and made it an easy decision for him.

'If you're doing nothing, would you mind helping me make the beds? And then there's a lot of tidying up and organising to do in the kitchen now that we can use it again.'

'Of course. But I was about to take Arthur for a walk.'

'Of all the excuses you have made to get out of helping me, that has to be the most unbelievable. You don't even like dogs.'

'Oh but I do, I do. Very much.'

'Bullshit. But he does need a walk. So go on then. But don't take too long. No stopping off for a quick pint.'

Barney attached the lead and headed to the common once again. There seemed to be fewer walkers out today. He wandered around for a while checking out various women but was wary of talking to any of them because of what happened last time. He was on the verge of going home when he caught a glimpse of a woman walking behind him with a dog. He couldn't get a clear look at her, but she appeared to be taking an interest in him. He played it cool and kept walking. But slowly. He was aware of her gaining on him. Could it be working this time? He was aware of her coming to almost touching distance. Then he jumped out of his skin when she threw her arms around him and kissed him on the cheek.

'Hello gorgeous.'

He was struggling to remain cool. Things had gone from one extreme to the other. Wait until he tells Liam about this one. He won't be laughing any more. He turned to get a proper look at her. Then it all became clear.

'Sue! What a surprise. Great to see you.'

'You too Barney. It must be what, ten years?'

'Eight and a half.'

Barney remembered it very well. He remembered it with resentment and regret. Sue made a suggestion.

'There's a pub not far from here called the Oddfellows Arms. Dogs are allowed in the beer garden as long as they're on a lead. Do you fancy a drink?'

'Yes. I certainly do.'

They arrived at the pub. Barney had never been in this pub before, which was unusual for him. He'd tried most of the pubs in the area. It was the sort of pub that was very much to his liking. It had a dartboard, pool table, sport on TV, and a large beer garden with a nice view. Little did he know that he would soon to be remembering this pub for other not so pleasant reasons. Sue ordered two pints and he asked her a question he instantly regretted.

'Do you come here often? What a corny line. What I meant to say was do you live around here?'

'Yes. About half a mile in that direction.'

'Wow. We're almost neighbours. I live three quarters of a mile the other way.'

'And in answer to your question, yes, I do come here often. Our darts team play their home games here. Do you still play darts?'

'No, not very often. I have the occasional game in Sunderland with my friend Neil if I'm up for a football match. But our team only plays once a year these days. We choose somewhere for a weekend away and fix up a friendly darts match with a local team. We've been to places such as Cornwall, York, St Andrews, Dublin. We had a great four days in Amsterdam. We're hoping one year to go to Las Vegas.'

'That sounds great. But it also sounds rather expensive. How do you afford it?'

'All of our players are millionaires.'

'Including you?'

'Oh yes.'

'Wow! That makes me even more frustrated that we didn't get together.'

'Not as frustrated as me. A combination of my mum and that clueless policeman ruined everything. I came back to try and find you the next day, but you'd gone. I was gutted.'

'I was somewhat disappointed myself. What's your situation now? Are you still single?'

'Np. I'm married and have a six-year-old son. How about you?

'I'm not married but I live with my partner.'

'A male partner?'

'Yes. Why?'

'Sorry. I shouldn't have asked you that. It's just something that happened to me a couple of years back on our trip to Cornwall.'

'Have you had your trip this year yet?'

'No. We usually go in the autumn.'

'Where are you going this year?'

'I'm not sure yet. Weve got a few ideas, but nothing definite yet.'

'Why not come here and play us? My team are a good bunch. It'll be a laugh.'

'Hey that's not a bad idea. I'll suggest it to the team, and I'll let you know. The only problem is two years ago I found us a team to play in Edinburgh and it wasn't a success. They might not trust my judgement again so soon. Our games are usually arranged by our captain Roy.'

'Why wasn't it a success? I've been to Edinburgh. It's a great place to have a drink.'

'There was nothing wrong with Edinburgh. It was the team we played against that were the problem.'

'What was wrong with them?'

'Nothing as such. They were just so boring. Not the sort who were ideal for hosting a drunken bunch like us on tour. They were called the Blood Donors. On the night of the match Roy made the mistake of asking their captain why they were called the Blood Donors. He spent the rest of the evening regretting it. Over the course of the evening, we learned everything there was to know about giving blood. I bet you didn't know you get given awards for the number of times you give blood. Right up to a thousand. Not extravagant awards. A certificate, a key fob and a badge maybe. None of that lot had got anywhere near that standard, but one of them was approaching his emerald award, which is 75 times. Two more of the team had already passed their gold award for 50 times. The rest of the team had all reached silver standard which was 25. That was the minimum requirement to play for their team. By contrast, when they asked how often our players had given blood it was a bit embarrassing.'

'How many times have you done it?'

'Just the once. But I fainted and felt really sick. It put me off doing it again.'

'You big wuss!'

'No, it wasn't like that. I didn't faint because I was squeamish. It was a reaction by my body to losing all that blood. They told me it was rare, but did happen occasionally, and tried to assure me that it probably wouldn't happen the next time. But I've not put it to the test.'

'What about the rest of your team?'

'Three of our team were rejected for various reasons. My wife Alison wasn't allowed because she had previously had a heart attack. Daffy was turned down because he had a low iron count in his blood. Ironically if he had been a woman he would have been accepted, but they have different criteria for males and females. I'm not sure why. Fiona was also rejected for medical reasons, but she didn't want to tell us the details. The rest of the team were in the category of always been meaning to do it but have never quite got around to it.'

'So your grand total was one donation? A donation that resulted in you toppling over and being sick.'

'I'm afraid so. Compared to their combined total of 325 for their team. You can sort of understand why they looked down on us.'

'You've got to give them a bit of credit. They might have been boring, but it's a very worthwhile thing to do, and they are right to be proud.'

'Oh absolutely. I'm not knocking them for doing it. It just made for a dull darts match.'

'Did you win the match?'

'No. I don't think we did. They weren't just better at us at giving blood. They were better than us at darts too. But we didn't care about that. As soon as the game was over, we were out of there and found somewhere more interesting.'

'Well if your team does take up my offer, I assure you we will provide a much more entertaining evening.'

'I would hope so. Ok, I'll put it to them and let you know.'

Barney bought them another pint each and they talked for another twenty minutes. He explained how the team had all become millionaires. He explained about the prank his lesbian friend and the rest of his teammates, and especially his wife played on him in Cornwall. Then they swapped phone numbers and Email addresses and went their separate ways. On the walk home he wasn't sure whether he was feeling happy or sad. Or a mixture of both. He was relieved that the dog walking experiment had finally come up with a bit of success. It was wonderful to bump into Sue again. But he couldn't help thinking what might have been if he hadn't been forced to leave the pub that night. Then another thought occurred to him. It wasn't just his mum and Sergeant Price that were to blame for wrecking his chances of romance that evening. The other members of her darts team also did their part to ruin things for him. Did he really want to meet them all again?'

14

It was Saturday morning. Barney didn't have any plans in particular. His Saturdays were usually spent having a few drinks and watching sport on the television. There wasn't anything special on today, but the weather was good so he might be able to have some time relaxing in the garden. The only snag was because it wasn't a school day he would have Jack for company. Alison had already told him she was going out in the afternoon. He didn't bother asking where she was going. It was usually shopping. She liked to do things the traditional way when it came to shopping. She actually went out to shops to do it. Barney was relieved about that. If she did her shopping online, he suspected their money would be all gone by now.

Watching Jack wasn't as difficult as it used to be. He could amuse himself quite happily. Alison had bought him all of the most expensive toys and devices, so he only tended to bother Barney when he wanted food. Alison gave him the usual warning about giving him too many crisps or sweets. As usual he would ignore it. She just about trusted him to take care of Jack, but never stopped reminding of the time when he cut all his hair off playing at being a hairdresser while Barney was watching the football results. She also regularly reminded him of the time Jack covered everything in the kitchen, including one of the cats with purple paint while Barney had briefly fallen asleep on the sofa. Jack was older now and would be happily engrossed with his toys, so Barney didn't have to do very much. But he thought it would be a good opportunity to talk to him about the things he had been telling the other children at school.

Alison left the house shortly after two o'clock. As soon as she had driven off Barney opened a bottle of red wine and sat down in his favourite spot. Jack was alternating between his trampoline, slide, swing, paddling pool, and everything else Alison had spoiled him with. Arthur was asleep on the ground next to him. The cats were out of sight like they had been for the majority of Arthur's visit. He had got used to the dog, without actually admitting to anyone that he had grown quite fond of him. But tomorrow he would be going back to his owners. Two hours passed serenely, and the bottle of wine was empty. That was always going to be the outcome. He never left a bottle of wine unfinished. When he got married and Alison brought all her belongings to their new house, and among them there was a stopper for a wine bottle. He'd never seen one before and they never used it once. He wondered what sort of person would come up with an invention like this. He imagined himself on Dragons' Den as one of the judges while one of the contestants attempted to pitch his idea.

'Hello. Tell me about your invention.'

'It's called a wine bottle stopper.'

'Intriguing. What does it do?'

'It stops the wine coming out of the bottle.'

'I don't follow.'

'Well, supposing someone opened a bottle of wine and had say two glasses from it. They could then put the stopper in it.'

'No. I'm still not getting it.'

'If you don't want to drink the rest of the wine you could save it for later.'

'Who would want to do that?'

'Er… I don't know.'

'That's got to be the stupidest invention I've ever heard of. You're fired!'

'That's a different show.'

'I don't care. You're still fired.'

Barney wasn't totally drunk but was on the tipsy side. He wanted more. He wandered off to the kitchen and opened another bottle. After a quick visit to the bathroom, he settled back into his chair with the second bottle. He recalled the recent conversation with his mum and gave the wine a spoof blessing using a bizarre selection of words. He wanted to see if it tasted better after he has turned it into the blood of Christ. He arrived at the conclusion that it did, and he gave it another blessing for good measure.

By the time Alison returned home and walked in with more bags of shopping than was feasible for a human being to carry without the use of a forklift truck, Barney was sloshed. As Jack seemed happy, she didn't give him too much of a hard time about it. In fact, she opened another bottle and poured herself a glass. Barney tried to bless it, but she told him to fuck off and not be so stupid. She took her glass inside and went to unpack her bags, dangerously leaving the third bottle within Barneys reach. At eight o'clock it was almost time for Jack to go to bed. Barney decided now was the time to talk to Jack, even though his was in no state to do so sensibly or comprehensibly. He wondered whether it was worth the bother. Jack never did what Barney told him. Then he had a wicked idea. A chance to cause some mischief and get revenge on that pain in the arse Mrs Solly. She only told him to tell Jack to stop saying those things. He would do that. It could hardly be his fault if Jack took no notice of his advice. He called him over.

'Jack. I need to talk to you about something.'

'Yes daddy.'

'You know when you told the children in your class there was a dead body in the kitchen? Well you mustn't do that again.'

'I won't.

'Good boy. Do you know where the body is now?'

'No daddy.'

'I moved it from the kitchen and buried it in the garden. Did you see me do it?'

'No.'

'Are you sure?' Maybe you did see me but forgot?'

'Yes daddy. I think I did.'

'Good boy. Now you mustn't go to school and tell anyone what you saw. Don't tell the other children.'

'I won't.'

'And especially don't tell Mrs Solly what you saw.'

'I won't.'

'Good boy.'

Alison came out to collect Jack and take him to bed. Barney was too drunk to move so she left him to it, still at the wine. It seemed to get dark all of a sudden, or more likely he had fallen asleep for a while. He had no idea of the time. He could hear a noise in the gloom. It was the dog panting with excitement and the sound of him digging frantically with his paws. He managed to force himself up from the chair and stumble towards where the noise appeared to be coming from. There was a secluded area at the bottom of the garden underneath some trees. It was very dark. Barney switched on the torch on his phone and lit up the area where Arthur was digging. He could see something sticking out of the ground. He went as close as he could get without toppling over. What he thought he could see looked like a bone. It had some sort of metal around it, like a bracelet. He stumbled back and stood in shock for a moment. The he wobbled his way back to his chair. He sat down and contemplated calling the police. But before he could do so he fell asleep.

He was awoken by the chirping of birds and the first sign of daylight. He felt awful. He called in to the kitchen for some paracetamol and a large drink of water. Then he went upstairs and climbed into bed. He was soon asleep again. When he woke up again the sun was shining through a gap in the curtains. Alison had already got up. He couldn't remember the conversation he had with Jack, but he vaguely remembered something at the bottom of the garden that somehow involved the dog. He quickly got out of bed and threw some clothes on. He rushed out to the far end of the garden. He could see it clearly now. There was a hole that Arthur had dug. Sticking out was a bone. There was a bracelet on it. He went back to the house and into the lounge where Alison was sitting. She could see he looked shocked.

'What's wrong?'

'You're not going to believe this. The dog has just dug up something in the garden.'

'What? What has he dug up.'

'It looks like a dead body.'

'Of course it is. I can't believe you're trying that one again. Do you really think I'm that stupid?'

'This is not a wind up. It's true this time.'

'Yawn.'

'Come and have a look if you don't believe me.'

'Yawn, yawn.'

Barney picked up his phone and called the police. After he answered a series of questions the call was ended, and he resumed the conversation with Alison.'

'You didn't really call the police, did you?'

'Yes I did. This is not a wind up. You'll soon realise that when they get here. I just hope they don't send that idiot Sergeant Prick.'

It wasn't long before the doorbell rang. Barney opened the door and much to his dismay, there stood the man himself. Sergeant Price.'

15

'Well well well. Look who we have here.'

'Policemen only say things like that in cartoons. And you must have known who you would have here. I gave my name when I reported it.'

'So you admit you were the one who reported it?'

'Yes. I do. I doubt I could get away with reporting something to the police and then denying it. Not that there could be any reason for doing such a thing.'

'You just can't stay away from trouble, can you. This is a serious matter.'

'Whoever is in charge at the station obviously doesn't think it's a serious matter. They wouldn't send a fuckwit like you to investigate a potential murder.'

'I'm not investigating a murder. I'm investigating a smartarse putting in a hoax phone call. Wasting police time is also a serious offence.'

'In that case you should have been prosecuted a hundred times.'

'You're intending to stick with this ludicrous story that you found a dead body?'

'I never said I found a dead body. I said I found something resembling a bone with a bracelet on it. You are jumping to conclusions.'

'So you're changing your story now?'

'No. I'm not changing it in the slightest. Far be it from me to tell you how to do your job, but why don't you go and have a look?'

'Don't tell me how to do my job.'

'What are you going to do then?

'I think I ought to go out and have a look.'

'What a brilliant idea.'

'You can be as clever as you want. But I've got a feeling you're going to get your comeuppance this time. Now show me where the garden is.'

'It's upstairs.'

'What?'

'We keep it outside like most people. But given that you couldn't find your arse with both hands, you'd better follow me.'

Barney led the way and Price followed him outside. On the way they passed three empty wine bottles.

'It seems you had a bit of a party last night.'

'No. Just a few quiet drinks.'

'Excessive alcohol consumption is a common reason for reporting fake sightings.'

'Some of us don't get pissed and make a dick of ourselves after a bottle of wine.'

The jibe visibly riled Price. He instantly realised Elizabeth must have told him everything, or nearly everything. He felt embarrassed. But he kept cool. He would get his revenge in good time. He finally got to the hole at the bottom of the garden and stared at it for a while, trying to give the impression that he was thinking. Then he turned to Barney.

'I am going to cordon off this area. It is now a crime scene. Do not enter it.'

He then walked briskly back to the house and out of the front door. He got in his car and drove off. Five minutes later the car was back. He got out and rang the doorbell.

'I forgot to take a statement.'

16

On Monday morning a team turned up to investigate the discovery at the bottom of the garden. There were four of them and they brought in a lot of equipment. The team leader suggested that they could be there for most of the day. Alison wanted to get out of the way, so packed her gym bag and headed off to the health club. Barney was also keen to get out of the house. He decided to send a text message to Sue and find out if she would be keen to meet up again. She answered immediately and certainly was keen. They arranged to meet in the Oddfellows Arms at 12.30. Barney wasn't expecting a major session, and it was drizzling, so he drove there. Sue was already there when he turned up at exactly 12.30. She already had a pint ready for both of them, so Barney sat down next to her. They didn't have dogs with them this time and also because of the rain they sat inside. It gave him a chance to get a good look at the pub. They chatted about nothing much for a short while, then she asked him a question which surprised him.

'What's your wife like?'

'Errm… She's alright.'

'Just alright?'

'Well. No. She's good.'

'You don't sound all that convincing.'

'That's probably because your question caught me off guard. I wasn't expecting it?'

'Are you not happy with your marriage?'

'I'm fine. We both are. We have our ups and downs like anybody else, but we're still together, so we must be doing something right.'

'That might be something to do with all the money you've got.'

'I don't think that's anything to do with it. Do you mind if we change the subject? It's making me a little uncomfortable.'

'Oh. I'm sorry. I guess I'm just a bit envious of other couples and their perfect relationships.'

'I never said it was perfect.'

'No. But It sounds better than mine.'

'I see. Aren't you happy with your partner?'

'Not at all. Horace is horrible to me. That's not his real name by the way.'

'That doesn't sound good. In what way is he horrible to you?'

'He doesn't let me do anything I want to do. He's controlling. He checks my phone. He tells me who I can be friends with. He tells me what clothes I should and should not wear.'

'Why do you stay with him?'

'Because I love him.'

'He doesn't come across as someone you could love.'

'That's not your business.'

'You brought up the subject. I was happy to talk about our proposed darts match. I'm really sorry to hear about your relationship.'

An uncomfortable silence followed. Then Barney took a chance and started the conversation again.

'Look, if it helps, my wife Alison was in a marriage which was just the same as your situation. Her first husband did all of those things your partner does. He wore her down with his endless bullying. She had lost all of her friends and became timid without any purpose in life. But one day she decided she wasn't going to suffer any longer and she was eventually strong enough to walk away. Now she's a strong woman. Sometimes even too strong. And happy too. I hope.'

'Good for her. Whoopie do.'

'I'm only trying to help. There's no need to be like that.'

'You don't understand. Horace can be nice. Sometimes.'

By now Barney was not enjoying the nature of this conversation at all. After a few minutes of another difficult silence, he tried to steer it in a slightly different direction.

'If you don't mind me asking, why did you call him Horace if that isn't his name?'

'That's just his nickname. His real name is John Hauskuller. His grandfather was German. When he was at school, the other kids kind of corrupted his name into Horace Horsecollar, who is a Disney character.'

Another awkward silence followed. Barney took the opportunity to go to the bar and get them another pint. When he returned, he managed to steer the conversation completely away from their relationships and on to something he felt more at ease with. They talked about the proposed darts match and the atmosphere became more bearable.

'Have you spoken with your team about this darts match?'

'Yes. They sounded keen. If we could pencil in a few dates, we can check with the pub to find out when the board is available and we'll get it organised.'

When they had finished their drinks, Sue headed for the bar again. Barney would normally limit himself to two pints if he was driving, but as it was only a very short drive, he didn't think it would matter. Then when they had finished those ones, he felt he ought to get another round in to make things even. He realised he most definitely should not be driving after four pints, even if it was only a short drive home. But it was still raining and he didn't want to get wet.

They came out of the pub and said goodbye, unaware that they were being watched. Then they headed off in opposite directions. Barney waited until she was out of sight before he got in the car. Then he drove off. He was feeling disappointed. Sue was a different person to the one he met last week. Or from the one he met years ago. She was asking some inappropriate questions about Alison. And she was unnecessarily aggressive towards him when they were discussing her own situation. He felt sorry for her because he was only too aware of what it must be like being in a controlling relationship having heard Alison describing her experiences.

He didn't have very long to dwell on it. He saw a police car in his mirror. He stayed calm. It was unlikely they were interested in him. But when he turned a corner the police car was still behind him. Then he recognised the driver. This had the potential to be a disaster. Price was going to get enormous pleasure in nicking him for driving over the limit. He had to think quickly. How was he going to get out of this? Luckily for him Price didn't take any action other than to follow him home. As he pulled into the street he had an idea. He pulled up outside the house and ran inside. He dashed into the kitchen and opened a bottle of wine. He poured a tiny amount into a glass and tipped half the bottle down the sink. What a waste. If only someone had invented some kind of device that you could put in the bottle that would allow you to keep half a bottle of wine for later, he might have already had half a bottle in the kitchen. The doorbell rang. He didn't do anything at first. It rang again and he slowly walked to the door. He opened it and there was Sergeant Price.

'Hello Mr Barnard. May I come in?'

'Of course you may Sergeant. What a pleasant surprise. How can I help you?'

'Have you been drinking?'

'Yes I have as a matter of fact. Why?'

'Because it's against the law.'

'Drinking is against the law? Since when?'

'Drinking and driving is against the law.'

'I knew that one. But I haven't been.'

'I saw you come out of the pub and drive home.'

'You were following me?'

'Only by coincidence.'

'I only had one pint in the pub.'

'We'll let the breathalyser decide that. Would you please blow into this?'

Barney did as he was told. Price inspected the test result and pretended to be surprised.

'Oh dear oh dear. It would appear you had more than just the one pint.'

'No. I only had the one. But I also had three glasses of wine when I arrived home.'

Priced looked at the half bottle of wine and was getting visibly frustrated.

'You've only been back for five minutes. You couldn't have drunk all that.'

'Yes I could. I'm a very quick drinker. Especially when I'm being unfairly harassed by the police.'

'Who were you with in the pub?'

'Nobody. I was on my own.'

'I saw you talking to a woman outside the pub.'

'She was just asking for directions.'

'What was her name?'

'I have no idea, Sergeant.'

'I don't believe you. I think you are lying to me.'

'Maybe it would be best if you stopped thinking. It's not your strong point.'

On that note Price stormed out of the door in a foul mood. Barney laughed out loud. He looked out into the garden and could see the people still at work. So he grabbed the rest of the wine bottle and sat in front of the television.

17

Alison and Barney were lying in bed watching the television. Barney had already taken Jack to school and left Alison to have a lie in. When he returned, he made them a pot of tea and took it up to the bedroom with some biscuits, then climbed back in. They didn't have anything planned for the day. Alison would be packing her suitcase for their holiday. She liked to pack well in advance. Barney usually left it until the last minute. The team of investigators seemed to have finished their work in the garden, but they had been warned not to touch anything.

'I hope Sergeant Prick doesn't turn up here again. He is becoming a right pain. And he seems determined to nick me for something. It's becoming an obsession.'

'You'd better be a good boy then.'

Alisons words were said in a suggestive tone. Barney didn't need a second invitation. He climbed on top of her.

'How about if I be a naughty boy?'

'I might have to punish you.'

Sadly, their impromptu erotic session was about to be thwarted. They had hardly got started on the foreplay stage when they heard the doorbell ring.

'Who the hell is that?'

'How would I know? Just ignore it. It's probably just a parcel delivery.'

'I haven't ordered anything. Have you?'

'No. I don't think so.'

They waited. The doorbell rang again. Barney got up and looked out of the widow. He saw a police car in the street.

'Oh bollocks. It's that twat again. This is getting out of hand. He is just going to keep hounding me until he can find some crime to fit me up for.'

Barney got out of bed and retrieved the clothes he had worn to take Jack to school. He had to wait a few minutes for things to subside before he put his trousers on. Then he went downstairs and opened the door.

'Morning Mr Barnard.'

'What do you want this time? This is starting to feel like harassment. What are you trying to pin on me this time? Fraud? Arson? GBH? Sheep rustling? Riding a bike without lights? Walking on the cracks in the pavement?'

'How about Murder?'

'Murder? Have you lost your mind?'

'I'm afraid not. We have a witness who claims they saw you remove a body from underneath your kitchen floor and bury it in your garden.'

'You really have lost your mind.'

'Wishful thinking I'm afraid. We received a phone call from a certain Mrs Solly. She alleges your son told his teacher and classmates at school that he saw you do it.'

Barney now vaguely remembered how in his drunken state had encouraged Jack to say those things. Now it was coming back to bite him.

'You can't use a story made up by a six-year-old as evidence. The judge would order the jury to laugh at you.'

'Maybe not. But you are now at the top of the suspect list. When the forensic report comes in, we will be back to see you. Meanwhile don't leave town.'

'I'm going to Egypt next week.'

'You can't.'

'I can. And I am. Contrary to what you might have seen on television the police don't have the power to stop people from leaving town. Or even the country. You need to get an order from a judge. And you're not likely to get that on the strength of a bit of fantasy from a six-year-old. Now if you've not got anything else, I've got some unfinished business upstairs. Close the door on your way out.'

'I'm going. But I'll be back. You are in serious trouble this time.'

Barney hurried back upstairs.

'What did he want?'

'He thinks I murdered someone. Now where were we?'

18

They were all flying from London Gatwick, which Barney wasn't all that happy about. He wanted to fly from somewhere closer to home. Such as Manchester. But there were various reasons that didn't work out, so Alison and Barney had no option but to make the long drive to Gatwick. They usually had at least one overseas holiday every year, but for Mary and Liam it was a rare treat. Alison had helped them out with some of the cost. Barney had begrudgingly agreed. But he was happy that they were coming too. Jack and Louis got on well and could keep each other amused and hopefully leave him in peace. He could have said the same for Alison and Mary.

Barney had drawn the short straw and was sitting next to Mary on the aeroplane. Liam had arranged it that way because he wanted to avoid sitting next to Mary or Barney. She didn't like flying, and her nervous state caused her to babble on for the whole journey. Barney in contrast preferred to enjoy a couple of beers in the airport bar then sleep during the flight. His fear of heights didn't apply to large passenger jets. He just didn't look out of the window. The only bit he didn't like was climbing the stairs on wheels that they use to board the plane from the tarmac, and he didn't have to do that at Gatwick as it had covered walkways to the aeroplanes. There was a chance he would have to face that on the return flight. Sadly, for him he wasn't likely to get the chance to sleep on this journey. Mary was waffling away before the plane had barely got off the ground.

'Are you looking forward to your holiday dickhead?'

'Mary. Can I ask you something? Why do you always call me dickhead?'

'Because you are one.'

Barney sighed.

'Cheers.'

'You're welcome. So what's the answer?'

'To what?'

'Are you looking forward to your holiday?'

Barney sighed again.

'Yes.'

'Have you ever been on an all-inclusive holiday before?'

'No.'

'Are you looking forward to it?'

'Christ, how many times are you going to ask me that?'

'No, what I mean is, are you looking forward to it being all inclusive?'

He sighed for a third time.

'I suppose so.'

'Why?'

'Well for a start, because everyone eats and drinks in their hotel, there shouldn't be loads of irritating British holidaymakers getting all excited because they've found an English or Irish pub and a fish and chip shop.'

'Why does that bother you?'

'Because what's the bloody point in going to all the expense and effort of going abroad when all you want is an English pub and a fish and chip shop. You might as well stay in Middlesborough, or Leicester, or go to Weston-Super-Mare or Great Yarmouth for your holidays.'

'But you aren't guaranteed to get the hot sunny weather in those places.'

'That's the other thing. British people go to somewhere hot, then moan that it's too hot.'

'You're not being nice about your own people.'

'Sometimes I'm ashamed to be British. Don't get me wrong. There are some very good people in our country. But there are also plenty of bad ones. And they all seem to go on holiday in the same place as me.'

'Oh come on. I'm sure they aren't that bad.'

But Barney was in full flow now.

'The worst ones are the xenophobes and racists who think black people are inferior to them, then they spend a fortnight lying on a sun lounger trying to turn their skin darker, even though they will probably just go red and give themselves wrinkles and skin cancer.'

'Sorry I asked.'

'You're welcome. Oh my god! What the hell was that?'

'What? What do you mean?'

'Did you not feel it? I'm sure I felt the plane wobble? And one of those engines doesn't sound right.'

'You'd better be fucking kidding me.'

'No. I think we're in a spot of trouble. I think there's a good chance that engine is going to catch fire and we are going to crash. Do you mind if I go to sleep now?'

'No! No you can't!'

Barney drifted off into sleep, while Mary sat there in fear. She knew deep down that Barney had just been winding her up when he said the engine doesn't sound right. She listened to the noise of the engines. She convinced herself Barney wasn't winding her up after all. The engines didn't sound right. She started to panic.

'Barney!'

No response. She increased the volume.

'Barney!'

Still no response. The volume went up even further. She was now shouting.

'Hey dickhead. Fucking wake up!'

Several heads turned and gave her disapproving looks. Barney jumped out of his skin.

'What the hell do you think you're doing?'

'Sorry. I'm scared. Did you mean it when you said there was a problem with the engine?'

'No, of course I didn't, you idiot. Do you seriously think I would just quietly drop off to sleep if I thought the plane might crash?'

'Yes. You probably would.'

'Do you mind if I go back to sleep now?'

'Yes, I do mind. The engine doesn't sound right.'

'Mary. You wouldn't know the difference between a perfectly good engine and one that was about to explode. There is nothing wrong with this aeroplane. The only horrible noises I can here are coming from you.'

'Thanks very much.'

'You're welcome. Can I go back to sleep now?'

'No. I need you to talk to me until this thing is on the ground.'

'Ok. What would you like to talk about?'

'Anything.'

'Cricket?'

'No.'

'Football?'

'No.'

'Politics?'

'No.'

'Vending machines?'

'Definitely not.'

'What then?'

'I don't mind. Anything.'

'How about work?'

'Okay.'

'How's work?'

'Boring.'

This was followed by a brief spell of silence. But Mary wasn't going to stay quiet for long.

'Would you return to work again if I had another crisis?'

'You must be joking. After what happened last time? No, my working days are well and truly over. Forever.'

'But you must have had some good times when you were working? I know you liked to moan about all of the pillocks you had to deal with, but you must have had some good times too?'

'Yes, it wasn't all bad. I made some very good friends over the years. But for some reason you remember the morons more.'

'Then tell me one of the high points you remember fondly?'

'Alright. Do you remember when we went to Windsor races? I had been fixing one of their coffee machines that morning and they were so grateful I had done such a good job they gave me two VIP tickets for the evening racing. They must have been worth at least a hundred quid for the pair. But it wasn't the money. It made such a nice change for someone to show a bit of gratitude for the work I'd done for them.'

'That's a nice tale. But I'm not used to you talking like this. I prefer it when you're slagging our customers off. Why don't you tell me one of the low points?'

'Alright. There is one job I did that springs to mind when I'm thinking of the bad times. It combines meeting one of the rudest people I've encountered at work, and there are many competitors for that particular title, and a moment when I struggled not to burst into tears.'

'That's more like it. Tell me all about it.'

'I was working in Great Ormond Street Children's Hospital in London. I was repairing a snack machine in one of the cafes. A nurse came up to me and started ranting and swearing at me. All because I had the audacity to be repairing the machine during her break. She didn't like the noise I was making and wasn't happy that she couldn't use the machine even though she wouldn't have been able to use it whether I was there or not because it was broken. Not only that, if I hadn't had been fixing it during her break, it would have presumably been someone else's break if I had done it at a different time. But the whole thing was put into context when I was approached by a woman who was crying her eyes out and managed to ask me for a bar of chocolate. I gave her the chocolate and she looked so distraught I found it hard not to cry myself. She took the chocolate and sat down at a table with a man who was also crying. I don't know exactly what devastating news they had just received, but this was a children's hospital, so I could only imagine. But this whole episode showed such a sharp contrast between people who have genuine reasons to be heartbroken and others who get hysterical over a vending machine being out of order.'

'That's awful. I know there are people like that I've had them on the phone often enough. I realise I can be a touch abrasive on occasions. And so can you. But I find it incredible how truly horrible some people can be. Maybe that's another one you will have to try to explain to your imaginary alien friend.'

'He's not imaginary. He's real. And I've got a lot of things to explain to him.'

'You are always mocking people who believe in God, yet you

say you believe in aliens. Isn't that a tad hypocritical?'

'No, not at all. Believing in gods is absurd. But it would be rather arrogant of the human race to think Earth is the only planet among trillions of other planets in the universe that has life. I don't know if there is life on other planets. But I find it difficult to rule it out.'

'It's refreshing to hear you believe in something. It makes a change from being so dismissive of things other people believe in.'

'Not at all. I believe in many things. For instance, I believe in gremlins.'

'Gremlins?'

'Yes, gremlins. I can see two of them right now, out there pulling bits off the wings.'

'And you wonder why I call you dickhead.'

Barney had always imagined that an alien would one day come to earth and ask him to explain some of the bizarre and odious behaviour of mankind. The alien eventually appeared before him on the day he died on his ninetieth birthday, when his heart failed during a penalty shoot-out involving Sunderland in the champions league final.

The plane touched down on the runway and Mary was relieved. Barney was even more relieved.

19

None of them had been to Egypt before. They soon discovered that it wasn't the sort of place where you could just wander around a pleasant little town or harbour popping into bars and restaurants, like you could in places such as Spain or Italy. There were plenty of organised trips to various historic buildings, pyramids and such, which Alison was keen on but none of the others were. They were on an all-inclusive deal, so they felt there was little point in going out as there were plenty of good bars and restaurants in the resort to keep them happy. Liam in particular was looking forward to eating as much as he wanted without paying for it. Barney was the same but swap eating for drinking.

They also discovered that there were plenty of activities arranged, which had advantages and disadvantages. Jack and Louis spent most of the days in kids' clubs, and they only ever saw them when they were hungry. But they also had to suffer an endless procession of holiday reps coming up to them and persuading them to take part in various events. Liam signed up for anything that was suggested to him. On the first morning he was off trying archery. He left Mary happily lying on a sun lounger trying to get a tan. Alison was less considerate to Barney and was continually pestering him to do something he had no interest in.

'Are you just going to lie there all-day drinking beer?'

'Your point being?'

'There are plenty of good things on offer. Why don't you try some of them?'

'I think your first idea of lying here all day drinking beer was a pretty good one.'

'But you would benefit from a bit of exercise.'

'The bar is a bit of a walk. That will be enough exercise for me. I'll be having a swim now and again. Maybe.'

'I'm doing aqua aerobics a bit later. Why don't you come along?'

'I don't know what that is.'

'It's exercises done in the swimming pool.'

'You mean swimming?'

'No. I mean aerobics. Done in the pool.'

'No thanks. I shall decline your kind offer.'

Liam went off to his archery and Alison to her aqua aerobics leaving Mary and Barney lying on the sun loungers. Yet another rep approached, and Barney didn't give her time to speak.

'Whatever form of entertainment you are going to offer me I am not interested. Nothing is going to move me from this spot for the rest of the day.'

'No problem. I'm just arranging the darts tournament. But not to worry. Just take it easy. Have a nice day.'

'Oh well, if you insist. Give me five minutes while I fetch my darts from the room.'

Mary looked at him with contempt.

'You brought your darts with you on holiday?'

'Yes I did. I take them everywhere with me.'

'Why?'

'In case of an emergency. Like this.'

'Won't they provide darts? I can't imagine anyone else has brought their own.'

'I hope not. That will give me a great advantage It's not easy to adapt to darts which are a different weight and length to the ones you are used to.'

'I hope you lose.'

'Thanks.'

He dashed back to the room, moving far quicker than was necessary to collect his darts and headed for the area where the darts were taking place. This was an unexpected bonus. Nothing could persuade him to do the archery, aqua aerobics, beach volleyball, water polo, chess, croquet, yoga, etc. But he could never resist a game of darts. However, he was disappointed when he saw the other competitors. There were seven kids aged between ten and fourteen years old, an elderly man who was the grandad of one of the kids, and two young women with eastern European accents. None of them appeared to know much about darts. But his competitive nature meant he would still try to win.

The game was a form of 'killer' which he had come across before. Everyone had a number and took turns in hitting everyone else's number until they had lost the five lives they started with. There was never any doubt in the outcome. He won easily. Then he wondered back to his sun lounger, quite chuffed that he had won his first overseas darts tournament.

The next morning the same rep asked if wanted to play again. He said he would, but he wouldn't be trying so hard this time. It would be nice if one of the others won. But because the others were so bad, he still won. He decided he wouldn't take part the next day.

The next morning the rep approached.

'Come on Barney. It's time for the darts.'

'No, not today. I'm going to give it a miss.'

All of a sudden, he was surrounded by the kids who played the previous days.'

'Come on Barney. You've got to play. Come on.'

They pulled at him and pleaded with him to come. He eventually gave in. But as he wandered off surrounded by the kids, he knew he had to lose. He decided to throw for bullseyes, which if hit knocked a life off everyone, but were more difficult to hit. The plan was working as he couldn't hit any, and it looked like one of the eastern European women or a thirteen-year-old boy would win. Then in one visit he hit two bullseyes. The rep took her stick of chalk and drew some lines through the contestant's names.

'You're out, you're out, you're out, and you're out. And the winner is Barney.'

The next morning, and for the rest of the week he stayed in his room until the darts started and managed to avoid taking any further part. In the afternoon Liam and Alison had finished their activities. Alison had been doing a keep fit session, this time on dry land, and Liam had joined in a game of water polo. Mary and Barney had just lazed about all day as usual. Now they were all together lying next to the pool. They were approached by a young lady who was one of the reps, and she was with a rather pompous looking man who didn't look happy. The man let the rep speak on his behalf, as if she was his solicitor.'

'Sorry to bother you, but are you the parents of Jack and Louis?'

Mary was the first to overreact.

'Yes. Oh my god! What's happened? Has there been an accident?'

'No no no. They are fine. I just need to speak to you about their behaviour at the kids' club.'

Barney, who as usual had been sampling the free beers all day stepped in.

'Hey, this is my specialist subject. Allow me to handle it. Now then. What have they been up to?'

'They pulled down the swimming shorts of this chap's son and threw him in the swimming pool.'

'Why did they do that?'

'I've no idea. But it is completely unacceptable.'

'I wish I had a quid for every time someone has said that about Jack. Just out of curiosity you don't happen to have a grandmother called Mrs Solly back in England, do you?'

Alison decided it would be better if she took over.

'I think the best thing to do would be to ask the boys why they did it. They're just over there.'

She called them over.

'Jack. Could you explain to Mummy why you pulled a boys swimming shorts off and threw him in the pool?'

Jack stood there looking sheepish and didn't answer. But Louis was much more eager to speak.'

'He was being horrible to Jack. He calls him a spaz, and a freak. He's been doing it all week.'

'That's not nice. But being called names can't hurt you. You should have just ignored him.'

'He also said his dad told him our parents were a bunch of chavs.'

Barney got involved again.

'Do you mean this lanky streak of piss here?'

He nodded towards the pompous looking man who joined in for the first time.

'I can see where your thug of a son gets his manners from.'

'And I can see where your snotty little brat gets his from.'

The rep tried to cool things down.

'Would you all mind keeping it civil? We do not tolerate this sort of behaviour at our resorts. I think it would be only right for the parents of Jack and Louis to apologise, and we can consider the matter closed.'

Mary was first to respond.

'Apologise. To this arsehole. He can fucking whistle for it.'

Liam chipped in.

'Now now my dear. There's no need to be like that. I will do the apology. I would like to say to this gentleman I am so sorry. Sorry that I wasn't there to see it. It must have been hilarious.'

Barney joined in the fun.

'I would also like to offer my apologies to the gentleman. I am sorry. Sorry that they hadn't emptied the water from the pool before they threw him in.'

'Why do they let riff raff like you come on holiday and ruin it for decent people? Why don't you go to Benidorm?'

This comment sent Liam over the edge.

'Riff Raff am I? Well let's see how you like this, your lordship.'

Liam grabbed him and pulled his shorts down, then dragged him towards the pool.'

'Don't you dare manhandle me. It's only fair to warn you that I was am a former Royal Marine.'

'That's handy Colonel Blimp. You should be able to fucking swim then.'

He threw him into the pool with his shorts around his ankles.

Later that evening Liam, Mary, and Barney were all pleased with themselves and had even more drinks than usual. They were expecting Alison to disapprove of their behaviour, but she had taken it surprisingly well. She was even quite secretly proud of their efforts in sticking up for their sons. She also wished she hadn't told Jack that being called names can't hurt you. That's what the teachers and her parents used to say to her when she was a schoolgirl. She didn't believe it then and she didn't believe it now. Verbal insults can be hurtful and she had explained that to the boys. They all regretted using bad language in front of the kids, but unfortunately in life you meet people now and again who cause you to lose it. The rep however had informed them that they were now banned from coming on any of their holidays ever again.

On the penultimate evening of their holiday, Barney and Liam were sitting at a bar overlooking the sea. Alison had somehow managed to persuade Mary to accompany her on one the organised excursions during the day, and when they got back they were both tired so went back to the rooms early with Jack and Louis. Liam, who had so often been a victim of Barneys ridicule was desperate to bring up the subject of Barney's dog walking antics.

'How is the dog walking going? Have you had any improvements on the gay geezer who tried to lure you back to his house? Or the posh woman who thought you were a pervert?

'As a matter of fact I have. Do you remember a few years back when I was up here visiting my mum and I met that girl Sue at the dartathon in the local pub, who I was getting on nicely with her until Sergeant Prick turned up and ruined everything?

'Yes. Vaguely.'

'I bumped into her while I was taking the dog for a walk. She lives not too far from us. We went for a drink, then I went for another drink with her a couple of days ago.'

'You old dog! I told you it would work. I don't suppose you mentioned it to Alison?'

'It's not like that. We just had a drink.'

'Don't dodge the question. Have you mentioned it to Alison?'

'No, not yet. But I will.'

'What's she like. Do you still fancy her?'

'Yes. No. She was very nice on our first meeting. But she was saying some strange things on our second encounter.'

'What sort of strange things?'

'She was asking questions about Alison and our relationship which I felt were inappropriate.'

'You'd better watch out for her then. Fatal Attraction and all that. Is she single?'

'No. And that was the other thing. Her partner Horace sounds like a right bastard. He is a control freak. She gets the same sort of treatment Alison had to endure with Kenneth.'

'Why does she stay with him?'

'That's what I asked her. She bit my head off and told me to mind my own business. But we've all come across people who stay in toxic relationships when everyone else can see they should end it. Also, this Horace is not only a bully. He's a bit of a weirdo too. He practices urophagia.'

'Are they the ones who voted leave or remain?'

'You may be thinking of Europhobia. I said urophagia.'

'Oh that. You're right. That is weird.'

'You don't know what it means do you?'

'No, of course I don't.'

'Neither did I until two days ago. I find it revolting. Put it this way. The people who do it drink something disgusting.'

'Oh, you mean real ale drinkers?'

'No, not quite as disgusting as that.'

'What do they drink?'

'They drink their own piss.'

'Yuk. Why would anyone do that?'

'They believe it has health benefits.'

'Does it?'

'I very much doubt it. Apparently, Madonna used to piss on her feet to cure athlete's foot, but I don't know if that's true, or whether it even works. Also, if you get stung by a jellyfish, you're supposed to get someone to piss on you to relieve the pain. There was an Argentinian footballer who played for Sunderland called Julio Arca who was stung by a jellyfish on a Sunderland beach. All his teammates pissed on his leg. At the time I thought it was just a prank. But then I saw it on an episode of Friends. Monica was stung by a jellyfish and the other friends pissed on her. Apparently, jellyfish stings are alkaline and urine is acidic so neutralises it and eases the pain.'

'I think I'd rather just take the sting.'

'Me too.'

'What sort of person would drink their piss?'

'Bear Grylls did, on telly and encouraged everyone else to do so. But that was all about survival in an emergency. Like if you get lost in the jungle or stranded on a desert island. The other name that cropped up on the internet of people who did it was Rolf Harris.'

'Isn't he that creepy looking Australian geezer who played with his didgeridoo? Didn't he have a criminal record?'

'Yes. It was called Two Little Boys, and it got to number one.'

That one went right over Liam's head. He didn't even know what a record was. He only knew CDs and downloads. He pondered for a moment.

'Why does this Horace geezer need to practice it? Is he not very good at it? I suppose it takes a while to get used to the taste.'

'No, when I say he practises it, I mean… never mind.'

On the final afternoon of their holiday, they were all sitting by the pool. None of them were doing any activities today. Liam and Alison were worn out from all the effort they had put in over the week. Barney and Mary still couldn't be bothered to make any effort. Jack and Louis had been expelled from the kids' club. Liam was reading a British newspaper.

'Where did you get that?'

'They have them in the reception. Not todays though. They are yesterdays.'

'Anything interesting been happening?'

'Nah. Not really.'

Barney looked at the front-page headlines. It said, "Body of Missing MP Found."

'What's that about a body been found?'

'Some MP that went missing seven years ago. They've found his body.'

'Where did they find it?'

'In someone's garden.'

'I mean where about in the country. Which county?'

'Don't worry. It wasn't anywhere near you. It was down south somewhere. Cumbria, I think.'

'Oh give me strength. Allow me to explain Liam. Cumbria isn't down south. Cumbria is where we live.'

'I thought you lived in the lake district.'

'We do. The lake district isn't a county. Cumbria is the county.'

Barney grabbed the newspaper from him and read the story. Barney remembered the MP in question. His name was Rupert Spiffington-Smythe. He was a former conservative who had been thrown out of the party following a string of controversial comments and expense fiddles. He was the sort of politician Barney despised. He was a very divisive figure with extreme views on homosexuals and ethnic minorities. He went missing seven years ago and was never found. Until now apparently. There wasn't too much information at this stage regarding the exact location of where his body was found. But Barney couldn't help wondering about whatever it was the dog had dug up in his garden.

20

In the police station Sergeant Price was feeling a mixture of annoyance and anticipation. A chief inspector and his team were on their way over from Manchester. He had a reputation for being one of the top murder investigators in the country. Although Price was feeling put out by being removed from the case, realistically someone of his rank was never likely to stay in charge of a murder investigation, especially one of a high-profile MP.

The chief inspector arrived at the station ahead of his team and introduced himself. Price was surprised at how friendly he came across. He was half expecting an arrogant know all.

'Hello, I'm Chief Inspector Barlocks. Nice to meet you, Sergeant.'

'And it's a pleasure to meet you too sir. I'm Sergeant Price.'

'I know. I remember you from that kidnapping case a couple of years ago. Nice job.'

Price was happy to keep taking the credit for solving the kidnapping, even though he hadn't actually done anything. It was handed to him on a plate. All he did was make the arrest.

'Thank you sir. Ironically the people involved in that kidnapping are the same people whose garden the body was found in.'

'Are they now? Interesting. Very interesting. I need you to fill me in on everything you know about this case so far. I would also like you to stay on the case if you can spare the time?'

'Absolutely sir. But I thought you were bringing your own team with you?'

'I am. But to be honest my sergeant is a bit of an arse. It will be more productive if I could get stuck in before he gets here. He's more of a hinderance than a help. Have you got time to fill me in now?'

'Of course. Would you like to step into my office?'

'No. I've got a better idea. Let's pop out to your local pub. I could do with a drink after my journey.'

Price didn't object. And he couldn't go against the wishes of a chief inspector. They wandered down to the Dog and Trumpet, and Barlocks got the drinks in. Price was feeling quite chuffed that the chief Inspector was including him in the investigation. He tried his best to show an interest without coming across as a crawler.

'It must be an exciting life just dealing with murders all the time.'

'You'd think so, wouldn't you? But let me tell you it's not anywhere near as glamorous as you see on the television. The likes of Morse, Linley, Taggart, Barnaby, Vera, Rebus, Frost, Luther, Marple, etc. etc., even Sherlock bloody Holmes are all portrayed as cool and tough. They are never fazed by some of the gruesome things they come across. That's not real life. Even after many years of doing this job I sometimes feel physically sick when I see the victims of a knife attack or someone who has been beaten to death. But there are so many police dramas with murder, viewers have become immune to the graphic shots of victims. The likes of Line of duty and Silent Witness have scenes that should be making people throw up, not sit down with their families together and have their tea while watching. If they had to go out and face the real thing, they would get a shock when they saw what it was really like. Television has a lot to answer for.'

Price got the feeling Barlocks was about to go into a long rant which he had obviously done before. He had no choice but to listen.

'The problem with television is it is so far removed from reality. For instance, take that Death in Paradise. Do you know how many murders have taken place in that small Caribbean island? 117! 117 murders. Does that sound like paradise to you? It sounds more like hell to me. And the islanders all wander around like nothing is wrong. If I lived there I wouldn't dare leave the house. Then the only police on the island close up the police station and all wander down to the bar together and have a jolly old laugh, despite having just seen a gruesome murder victim half an hour earlier. And the vast majority of the murderers are British. Why don't they just stop allowing British people to live there. It will cut down their murder rate by 100%.'

'I see what you mean sir, and…'

'And as for that Midsomer Murders. Do you know how many murders they have had there? 423. Plus another 250 attempted murders. Who would want to live there? I'd expect to see for sale signs outside all the houses. But they just continue their lives as if nothing has happened. They all wander down to the village fete even though there is always someone killed every time they have one. The inspector goes home to his wife after a day of investigating brutal murders. Hello dear did you have a nice day. Yes dear. Not too bad. Mr Brown next door had his head hacked off by an axe wielding maniac. Oh what a nuisance. He was due to judge the marrow growing contest on Saturday. Never mind. Maybe his wife could judge it instead. But don't you remember his wife was strangled last week as she was taking her dog for a walk and then had her eyes poked out. Oh of course. What a silly billy I am.'

'Yes sir. I must confess, I don't really watch…'

'And another thing. The murderer is never the obvious suspect. It is always the last one you would suspect. In real life the obvious suspect is usually the one who did it.'

'I see what you are…'

'And the worst thing of all. The television detectives always solve the murder. They never have cases where it remains unsolved. Those smartarses always figure it out. How much pressure do you think that puts on us real life coppers?'

'I…'

'Exactly. And another thing. Have you ever seen Father Brown? Or the Sister Boniface Mysteries? They've got a bloody vicar solving murders. And a nun. And they make the policeman look arrogant and dim-witted. And don't get me started on Jonathan fucking Creek.'

Price decided he might as well just stay quiet.

'And another thing. There seems to be a trend of people writing books, such as Richard Osman with his Thursday Murder Club, and Robert Thorogood and the Marlow Murder Club. The murders are solved by a bunch of old age pensioners who investigate crimes as a hobby when they should be doing gardening or knitting or whatever it is pensioners get up to these days. Yet again making the police look stupid.'

There followed a few minutes of silence and they both took a large swig of beer. Much to the relief of Price, Barlocks had ended his rant. He returned to the matter in hand.

'Ok Sergeant. Tell me what you know about this case.'

'The body, which we believe to be that of Rupert Spiffington-Smythe, the MP who went missing seven years ago has been found in a garden belonging to a certain Cecil Barnard.'

'Why do they think this body is that of Rupert Spiffington-Smythe?'

'At the moment it's purely on the strength of the bracelet. It's exactly like the one he famously could be seen wearing every time he was on television.'

'And who is this Cecil Barnard?'

Someone who I have had dealings with in the past. I suspect he knows more than he is telling us.'

'I see. Has he had any criminal convictions?'

'Not as such.'

'Not as such?'

'No. He doesn't have any.'

'Why do you think he may be involved?'

'An eyewitness told us he saw Barnard burying the body in his garden.'

'That's somewhere we can start. Where can we find this eyewitness?'

'He's probably just coming out of school at the moment.'

'School? So he's a teenager?'

'No not quite. He's at primary school.'

'Exactly how old is this eyewitness?'

'I believe he is six sir.'

The chief inspector rolled his eyes. For the first time he wondered if he had overestimated the abilities of Sergeant Price. But for the moment he gave him the benefit of the doubt.

'I think I need to go and introduce myself to this Cecil Barnard.'

'I must warn you sir, he can be a right pain in the arse.'

'Don't worry sergeant. I'm sure I've dealt with a lot bigger pains in the arse than this chap. Maybe it would be a good idea for you to come along and sit in the interview room. I'll show you how it's done.'

'You're bringing him in?'

'Of course. Even the most arrogant of suspects are going to feel a little less comfortable being interviewed in the police station than they would at home. Besides, this is a murder investigation. We need to show him we mean business. Come on. Let's go and get him.'

21

It was a long, slow journey back home from Gatwick. Mary had invited them to stay overnight in Winchester, but they declined the offer. They just wanted to get back home, and they had things they needed to do the following morning. Barney had spent most of the journey grumbling that they should have flown from Manchester airport. Alison had occasionally nodded off, and when she was awake kept glancing across at the speedometer. She no longer would directly tell him that she thought he was driving too fast. Instead, she dropped subtle, and sometimes not so subtle hints. 'There seems to be a lot more of these smart motorways these days.' Or 'I wonder why they made this road a 60 mph limit.' Or 'The trees seem to be whizzing past today.' Or 'Did I tell you my friend Sonia has to do a speed awareness course?' Barney generally ignored her for as long as he could remain cool about it. Alison was reluctant to directly criticise him following an incident last year. On that occasion following a prolonged period of nagging him to drive slower, he drove the car into a service station, got out and told her that if she was such a great driver she could drive the rest of the way. He left her with no choice but to drive the remaining 130 miles home. She didn't want to take the risk of that happening again.

They arrived home shortly after 1 am. They went straight to bed, and it wasn't long before Alison was asleep. Barney couldn't sleep, even though he was exhausted. There was something on his mind. He couldn't stop thinking about the discovery of the body of the missing MP. And the discovery of whoever, or whatever it was in his garden. He felt it was absurd to think the two things were connected. But it made him feel uneasy all the same.

He turned on the television and turned to BBC News. It didn't take long for them to mention the MP, but there was very little new information. The police had not yet released the circumstances and whereabouts of the discovery of the body, although they were under increasing pressure to do so. He turned the television off and fired up his laptop instead. He wanted to find out more about this man.

Wikipedia revealed that Rupert Spiffington-Smythe had a grandfather, Henry Spiffington-Smythe, or otherwise known as Lord Spiffington-Smythe. He was involved in the coalmining industry in Yorkshire and had a reputation for cruel treatment of workers. He also attended the House of Lords, mainly to serve his own ego and to collect the allowance he was paid just for turning up. He had a son, Tarquin Spiffington-Smythe who he didn't get on with. Tarquin was sent away to boarding school where he was bullied because of his famous father and his ridiculous name. After he left school, he also left home as soon as he could. He changed his name to Thomas Smith and married a devout Catholic girl. They had a son they called Robert. Thomas had the complete opposite political views of his father. He became active during the miners' strike and was arrested twice for assaulting police on the picket lines. Robert was ashamed of this, and combined with his mum forcing God and Jesus down his throat every five minutes he couldn't stand it at home and as soon as he could went to live with his grandfather who he had always looked up to. He changed his name from Robert to Rupert and took his father's original surname.

His Grandfather had influence in the Conservative party,

mainly because of his donations, and had pulled a few strings to get his grandson to stand for parliament in a safe tory seat. He was duly elected but was soon in trouble for his outrageous speeches attacking immigrants, gays, women, elderly, and the disabled. He was thrown out of party after being caught fiddling his expenses. Barney decided he would use this example to explain British politics to his alien friend. They were happy to keep him as an MP despite his vile views but expelled him for doing what most of them did themselves. He then stood at the following election as an independent candidate. Extraordinarily he won because there was an astonishing amount of the public who agreed with his hate filled views. He continued as an MP for another two years after that election, and then just disappeared without trace.

Barney couldn't read any longer and fell asleep slumped in the armchair. He despised the man and his abhorrent views but had a tiny bit of sympathy for him. He knew only too well what it was like having a mother who was banging on about God and Jesus all the time. What it didn't tell him in Wikipedia was what a huge influence Rupert Spiffington-Smythe's mum was going to have on her son's life.

He didn't manage to get back to bed. He slept all night in the armchair and was woken up when Alison came downstairs and opened the curtains.

22

Kenneth wandered out of the prison gate. Or to be more accurate he hobbled out of the prison gate. He had never fully recovered and was unlikely ever to following the ferocious blow to his kneecap with a cricket bat by Alison. There was no one there to meet him. He felt lost. Prison had been his home for the past two years. He hadn't even served half his sentence for kidnapping his former wife. He hadn't expected to be released this early. He had always been a loner, but he was never on his own in prison. He was nobody out here. Inside he was somebody. Kidnapping didn't have the same stigma as sex offences or child abuse. He'd been beaten up a couple of times but didn't really mind. It was all part of being a notorious criminal. His first feelings of freedom were that he didn't want it. He could happily turn around and go back inside. He had ideas of committing another crime, but perhaps he ought to wait a while to see if he felt the same in a few days. He also had thoughts about getting revenge on Alison and Barney. But that could wait. He will get them one day.

He returned to his flat which had stood empty for two years. It didn't feel like home. He opened the windows to let some fresh air in. He had never felt so alone in his life. Then he remembered his favourite way of amusing himself when he was feeling lonely. He fired up his laptop and logged in to Facebook. After reading a few posts, and trolling a few people, he wasn't getting the kicks he used to from posting inflammatory comments. But a conversation about the discovery of the body of Rupert Spiffington-Smythe caught his interest. It didn't look as if grammar, punctuation and spelling of the British public had improved very much during his two-year absence. Or intelligence for that matter.

'im glad they found him dead he was evil.'

'not al of us are glad his dead some of us agree with hes points of view.'

'what you mean rasisem sexisem and homafobia.'

'hear come the woke brigade.'

'Whatever happened to free speech. You arnt allowed to say anythink these days.'

'I think he was a grate man.'

'I don't Im glad hes dead.'

'i think there should bring back the death pelanty.'

'A bit over the top don't you think.'

'no he deservs it.'

'But he's already dead. So even if the death penalty was brought back it's unlikely he would be sentenced to it. Especially for just making comments.'

'well I think if you are nd can think it should or might not so.'

'What the hell are you talking about?'

'here come the grammer police again.'

'It's nothing to do with grammar. What you just wrote was just a meaningless load of shit.'

'you are just so rued is they any need to be so rued I am entitelled to my opinion same as you theys no nee to be so rued.'

Kenneth thought this would be a good point to stir people up and see if it gave him the same thrill he used to get from it.

'I think Rupert Spiffington-Smythe was a great man. I agree with everything he said. The unemployed should be made to do national service, gays should be shot, sex offenders should have their balls chopped off in public without anaesthetic, blacks sent back to their own countries, and women belong in the kitchen, not in the workplace.'

Then he sat back and watched as the outrage poured in. It gave him a little satisfaction, but not the level it used to. He turned off the laptop. He needed to think about what to do next with his life.

23

Barney and Alison were taking it easy after returning home from their holiday. That's the trouble with holidays. You usually need another one to recover from the first one. Unlike Mary and Liam, they were fortunate that they didn't have to go back to work as soon as they returned. Jack was back in school, and they were having a lazy day watching television.

They were watching a recording of Richard Osman's House of Games from the previous evening. It was just about the only television programme they enjoyed watching together. Even so, they would often end up arguing about the answers. They used to watch the 1% Club, but Alison put a stop to that. She could no longer put up with Barney's rants about how stupid the people were who went on there, even though she generally agreed with him.

Alison had the remote control and kept pressing the pause button, so she had more time to think of the answers. This riled Barney. On the other hand, she was getting pissed off with him because he kept shouting out the answers before she had a chance to work them out. She was also getting fed up with him slagging off the contestants, especially the ones who he'd never heard of and questioned why they should be called celebrities.

'Who are these people? I only know the tennis player. I've no idea who the other three are.'

'They probably don't know who you are either.'

'Come on then. Do you know them?'

'Yes. One of them is a presenter on a house renovation show. Another one is a dancer on Strictly Come Dancing.'

'What about that odd looking guy on the end?'

'Ok. I admit I don't know him.'

The first round was called Rhyme Time. Richard Osman explained how it worked.

'OK. Fingers on buzzers. I will ask you two questions. Buzz in when you know the answers. But the two answers must rhyme. Here's your first one. What is a drink of whisky with ice, and what is a device for telling the time and makes a noise like a bird?'

None of the contestants pressed their buzzers.

'Nobody? The answers are Scotch on the Rocks and Cuckoo Clocks. Now you see how it works, here's your next one. What is the name of the actor who played Basil Fawlty in Fawlty Towers, and what is a dairy product you can put on toast to make Welsh rarebit?'

The home renovation show presenter buzzed in.

'Is it John Cleese and butter?'

'No, I'm afraid it's John Cleese and cheese. Don't forget the answers have to rhyme.'

Barney shook his head and tutted loudly.

'That woman is useless. She doesn't even understand how the games work. If I was going on a quiz show I would watch as many episodes as I could in order to avoid embarrassing myself in front of the whole country by not knowing the rules.'

They came to a round called Distinctly Average where the

contestants had to guess a number to a usually tricky question and the points go to whoever was nearest. The first question asked how long the M6, Britain's longest motorway was. Alison paused the screen and took time to think. Then she suggested it could be about 160. Barney responded by saying it might be closer to 200. Maybe even 220. The tennis player guessed first. He held up his tablet first which read 165. Alison got all excited and waved her arms in triumph. Barney spoiled her moment.

'It doesn't mean you're right. You could be both wrong.'

'Oh shut up.'

The presenter on the house renovation show held up her answer. It said 45. Barney shook his head again in disbelief.

'45? What an idiot. You seriously think that the longest motorway in the country is only 45 miles long?'

Then it was the turn of the dancer. Her tablet displayed 900. Barney went into meltdown.

'Oh my god! 900? The whole country isn't even that long. Where do they get these people from?'

'Don't get so wound up about it. Richard Osman obviously also thinks those answers are ludicrous, but he takes the piss out of them in a more subtle way.'

'You mean in a smug way.'

'I think he's very funny.'

'I don't like him.'

'Why not? He's very funny. Especially when he's a guest on Have I Got News For You.'

'I admit he's okay on that. But I don't like the way he writes a book and straight away it sells a million copies just because he's already famous. I bet if I wrote a book, it wouldn't sell a million. Even if it was better than his.'

'You couldn't write a book to save your life.'

'Well one day maybe I will.'

Richard Osman gave the answer. It was 230. Now it was Barneys turn to be smug. The next question asked how much in US dollars did the world's most expensive sculpture sell for. The contestants were again way off the mark, but so were Alison and Barney this time. The answer was $141 million for something called Pointing Man by Alberto Giacometti. This would normally trigger another rant from Barney about how many starving children could be fed with $141 million, and Alison would have agreed with him on this one. But he didn't get the chance. They heard the doorbell ring. Alison paused the television and went to see who it was. She came back looking serious.

'There're two policemen at the door. They want to speak to you. One of them is your friend Sergeant Price.'

'Not again. What they hell do they want this time?'

Barney went to the door to invite them in. But they didn't come in. Barlocks spoke first.

'Hello Mr Barnard. I am Chief Inspector Barlocks. I believe you already know my colleague, Sergeant Price. I'm afraid I have to ask you to accompany us to the police station.'

24

Horace was in a bad mood. Or at least Sue thought he was. Sometimes it was hard to tell. Sometimes he could be so nice to her, or at least that's what she imagined in her deluded mind. She had to be careful because any little thing could make him angry again. He'd been going through her phone again as he often did. Then she knew what would be coming next. Questions. Ridiculous allegations. Then she would have to give him explanations and try to justify her sins which were purely part of his jealousy fuelled imagination.

'Who is this Barney in your contact list? I've never seen his name in there before.'

'Oh, that's just someone I'm arranging a darts match with.'

'Have you been seeing him?'

'Don't be silly. No. I have only met him once at a darts match.'

Luckily Sue had remembered to delete all of the messages between her and Barney from when they arranged their recent meet up in the pub.

'Why do you need his number?'

'I told you. I'm arranging a darts match with his team.'

'You don't normally arrange your team's darts games. I thought Steve arranged all your matches.'

'Yes, he does usually. But I am arranging this particular one. It's not a normal league match. It's against a team that just wants to play a one-off friendly game.'

'So why are you arranging it and not Steve?'

'Because it was easier for me to deal with Barney.'

'Why?'

'Well I just bumped into him one afternoon while I was walking the dog and I remembered him from the Children in Need dartathon a few years ago.'

'You've just told me you'd never met him.'

'No I didn't. I said I only met him that one time. I haven't met him since.'

'It all sounds a bit suspicious to me.'

'No. There's nothing to worry about. I promise.'

Sue was relieved when he finally stopped questioning her. It was wearing her down, this relentless interrogation. But she didn't want him to be upset. She loved him. At least that's what she kept telling herself. She just couldn't see how bad he was treating her.

But Horace wasn't satisfied with her answers. He had the feeling there was much more to this Barney than she was telling him. He needed to find out. He was determined to find out. Once he had given her permission to leave the room, he looked at her phone again and this time delved deeper. He found a folder which was just named Darts. In there he found an address. And he was shocked to find out it wasn't very far from where they lived. That was all the proof he needed. There was something going on and he was determined to get to the bottom of it. He was going to find this Barney character.

25

Barney had been in a lot of police stations over the years, usually to make sure the boys in blue could buy a cup of coffee or a packet of crisps. Vendetta had vending machines in most of the police stations around the country. They were usually old buildings, built in Victorian times and had a distinctive feel and smell to them. This one didn't smell like the other ones. It had a different aroma altogether.

Price led the way up some stairs towards an interview room. At the top of the stairs, they were hit with the most horrendous smell. Barlocks had to fight hard to stop himself being sick.

'What the hell is that smell? It's revolting.'

'I don't know sir.'

But Barney knew. He pointed at the coffee machine in the corridor. It had a Vendetta logo on the front.

'That's your culprit. It has clearly been neglected. There is a waste bucket inside which collects the drips, and also the remains of drinks that people tip in there when they don't want them, despite the sign on the front that asks them not to do it. If it isn't emptied regularly it starts to smell. That one hasn't been emptied for a long time. It's the sour milk that gives it that lovely scent.'

'How come you know so much about vending machines?'

'How come I know so much about vending machines? That's like asking Stradivarius if he knows anything about violins.'

He pointed at the Vendetta logo on the front of the machine.

'I used to work for these lot for many years.'

'Do you have a key for it?'

'Why yes. I carry a big bunch of vending machine keys with me wherever I go. You never know when you might need them.'

'The Sergeant warned me about your sarcasm. Well it doesn't impress me. I've dealt with bigger smartarses than you.'

'I've probably got one in my garage at home. I'll just go back and dig it out then I'll pop round in the morning with it.'

'Nice try. You're going nowhere sonny.'

Sergeant Price intervened.

'I've seen the people working on this machine. They don't use keys. It opens electronically. They type in a code number, and it pops open.'

Barlocks turned back to Barney.

'Do you know the code number?'

He tapped the logo again.

'Of course. I used to work for these lot for many years.'

'Then would you kindly tell me what it is?'

'No. I can't do that. It would be unprofessional, and even unethical. I can't divulge confidential information such as that. Besides, how do I know you're not going to come back later and steal all the money?'

'Then just open it yourself and empty that fucking bucket.'

'I couldn't possibly do that either. I don't work for them any longer. Not only would that be unethical, but it might also even be illegal. I wouldn't want to be breaking the law. Especially with all these policemen around.'

'You'd be happy to put up with that vile smell just to spite us?'

'It doesn't bother me. I've become immune to it after working on them for more than thirty years. As for spiting you. Why on earth would I want to do that? I enjoy being forced to leave my home in the middle of Richard Osman's House of Games and get dragged down the police station by a pair of halfwit coppers.'

They realised they were wasting their time trying to get him to help. So they ushered him into the interview room and left him sitting there.

They had kept him waiting in there for what seemed like ages. This was all part of the tactics Barlocks was using. Get the suspect agitated and more vulnerable. Get him to say something he didn't want to. He was a seasoned professional. He wasn't about to let some smart alec get the better of him. He eventually walked into the room along with Sergeant Price.

'Hello Mr Barnard. Allow me to formally introduce myself. I am Chief Inspector Barlocks.'

'Pleased to meet you Chief Inspector Bollocks.'

'I said Barlocks.'

'What a dynamic duo we have here. Chief Inspector Bollocks and Sergeant Prick. They ought to make a television series about you. It would make a great comedy. Just like that one with Jasper Carrott and Robert Powell. That was about a pair of clueless policemen too. They could call it Cock and Balls.'

Barlocks stayed calm and planned to get his revenge later. Price wondered how long the chief inspector would keep his cool.

'There's no point in trying to be clever with me. It would be in your best interest to answer my questions in an honest and straightforward manner. Nothing else is needed. Is that clear?'

'Yes.'

Barlocks started by showing him a photograph of Rupert Spiffington-Smythe.

'Do you recognise this man?'

'Yes.'

'Would you care to enlarge on that?'

'No.'

'I would prefer it if you would.'

'You asked me if I recognised him. I said yes. Then you asked me if I would care to enlarge on it. I said no. I can't give more honest and straightforward answers than that.'

'Tell me what you know about him.'

Barney didn't say anything.

'Well?'

'Well what?'

'Tell me what you know about him.'

Barney said nothing.

'So now you're giving me the silent treatment?'

'Not at all. You didn't ask me a question. You just gave me an instruction. You didn't say anything about me following instructions. You just told me to answer your questions. Incidentally could you answer one of mine. Am I under arrest?'

'Let's just say you're helping us with our enquiries for now.'

'Then am I free to leave?'

'That wouldn't be in your best interests. I could easily charge you with murder. Then you wouldn't be going anywhere in a hurry. So how about we get on with it?'

'Yeah, alright.'

Barlocks held the photograph up again.

'Tell me what you know about this man.'

'He was a weasel faced flag shagger who spouted inflammatory crap to his hate filled jingoistic and racist followers. Even the Conservative party couldn't stomach him. That tells you how bad a person he was.'

Barlocks didn't like that. He was a Conservative voter. Price didn't mind it so much. He usually voted for the Liberal Democrats.

'You didn't like him much then. So motive is not going to be a problem.'

'Along with a few million others. That's a lot of murder suspects. I hope you've got a very large venue for the identity parade.'

'I noticed you said 'was' not 'is'. That means you are aware he is dead then? Interesting.'

'No. I had no idea he was dead. I've spent the last month living with a tribe in the Amazon rain forest in a mud hut without telephones or internet, with my hands over my eyes and my fingers in my ears.'

'How can you have your hands over your eyes and your fingers in your ears at the same time?'

'It's interesting you should ask that. The people in this tribe are very different to us. Their eyes and ears are so close together that they can actually do that. The other unusual thing about them is the males all have two penises. Apart from the tribe leader who has five. His underpants fit him like a glove.'

'Well lucky them. Can we get on?'

'No, they're not lucky really. Because all the females have three vaginas. So they live in a constant state of sexual frustration. A bit like your wife I would imagine.'

Price sensed that Barlocks was about to erupt.

'I can take all the bullshit from you, but if you say another thing about my wife, I promise you, you will regret it.'

'Sir, might I suggest we take a ten-minute break? I could do with a coffee. Would you like me to bring you one?'

'It depends. Where will you be getting the coffee from?'

'There's a vending machine on the… Oh, perhaps not.'

'No Sergeant. I think I'll give the coffee a miss, on the grounds that I don't want to catch some horrible disease. Now can we get on?'

'Yes sir.'

'Right Mr Barnard. We shall continue. I believe you discovered human remains buried in your garden.'

Barney said nothing.

'Well?'

'Very well, thank you.'

'Answer the question.'

'You didn't ask me a question. You just gave a statement. Again.'

'Don't start that again.'

'I am merely following your instructions.'

'Okay. Let's try it this way. Did you discover human remains in your garden?'

'I don't know.'

'What do you mean you don't know?'

'I discovered what looked like a bone with some sort of bracelet on it. I couldn't possibly confirm whether it was human or not. It might have been a dog or something. The people around here can be weird sometimes. They like to give their dogs strange haircuts and make them wear items of jewellery. Besides, it was the middle of the night, so it was very dark, and I was as pissed as a fart.'

'Well I can assure you it certainly was a human. The forensics team confirmed as much.'

'So why are you asking me?'

'Look Mr Barnard. You can continue with this attitude of yours and the whole process will take a lot longer. We are going to do this one way or the other, and we are going to stay here until you answer my questions, so it would be in your best interest to cooperate and stop trying to be clever.'

'I suppose you're right. I have been acting like a prat. From now on I'll make the effort to be a bit more helpful.'

'Thank you.'

'And I'd like to apologise. I shouldn't have said your wife was sexually frustrated.'

'No. You shouldn't have.'

A moment of silence followed. The calm before the storm.

'In fact, I wouldn't be surprised if she was getting some at this very moment, what with you being out of town and all.'

Barlocks exploded. He jumped to his feet and yelled at Price.

'Right! I've had enough of this. Charge this bastard with murder. Then lock him in a cell. We'll continue the interview in the morning.'

Barlocks stormed out of the room and price followed.

'Sir, you do realise you were recording this interview? It might not look good.'

'Sergeant, you have a lot to learn about police work. I've done this sort of thing before. I know a few tricks. Give him his phone call. Then lock him up.'

26

Alison was feeling was feeling nervous and she didn't know why. She had stayed at home while Barney had been away many times before and it hadn't bothered her in the slightest. But for some reason this time was different. She had been a strong character in her younger days. She would happily argue with someone who disagreed with her opinions and didn't back down from an argument. Then she found herself in a marriage where she was bullied and controlled and became a shadow of her former self. She became weak and timid, not just in the company of her husband, but with her work colleagues, and the few friends she was still allowed to socialise with. But once she had escaped from it she had become even stronger with a huge determination never to get in a situation like that ever again. This sometimes resulted in her being a bit bossier than she would like to be. Barney accepted it mostly in good spirit. He knew what she'd been through. And he liked people to have strong opinions.

Right now she needed some of that strength, but she wasn't feeling it. She was feeling more like how she did when she was in her oppressive first marriage. She had received the call from Barney telling her that they weren't letting him out tonight. Now she was jumpy. She knew he wasn't a murderer. He often expressed how he would like to murder certain people, but she knew he wouldn't actually carry it out. That means there is someone still out there who is. She dashed to the front door to check it was locked. When she was behind the door, she was sure she heard footsteps. It sounded like someone was running away. She told herself not to be so silly. It was just her imagination. All the same she went up to the bedroom and turned off the lights. She peeped out of the curtains and again she was sure she saw a shadowy figure duck behind the dustbins. Now she was scared.

She sat on the end of the bed wondering what she should do. Was it all in her imagination? Yes, it must be. But then she heard another noise. This time it came from around the back of the house. Like someone was trying to climb the garden fence. She couldn't take it any longer. She picked up her phone and dialled 999. They would surely take her seriously and come quickly. Especially with a young child in the house.

It was twenty-five minutes before they arrived, but it seemed like a lifetime to Alison. There were two of them, and for a change neither were Sergeant Price. One of them sat down and asked her a few questions. The other one had a look out of the widow in the kitchen overlooking the back garden.

'Now then madam. Could you describe what you think you saw or heard?'

'I heard someone running away from behind the front door. Then I saw someone hiding behind the dustbins. Then I heard someone climbing over our garden fence.'

'Are you sure?'

'Yes. I think so.'

The policeman obviously didn't believe her. But he was writing it all down as a matter of routine. But then they were interrupted by his colleague who came rushing in from the kitchen.

'I think I've just seen someone in the garden.'

They asked Alison if there was a light for the garden and she showed them where the switch was. They told her to wait until they were outside, then to hit the switch. She followed their instructions and when the garden was illuminated, they heard the sound of someone panicking and trying desperately to hide. They walked down to the bottom of the garden and saw a man lying in the very spot where the dead body was discovered.

27

By the time morning arrived, Barney was regretting his bad attitude during the interview. He had no intention of spending another night in custody, so he reluctantly secured the services of a solicitor. He wasn't going talk to the police again without him present. Barney didn't care much for solicitors. He thought they were just getting rich on the back of other people's misery. He didn't believe they really cared about their clients. They just wanted to win their cases for their own satisfaction. But he knew he needed one right now, and he was going to have to get on with him. He arrived just before noon and Barney was allowed out of his cell and into an interview room to meet him.

'Hello Mr Barnard. I am Brian Hadaway. Pleased to meet you. My associate Mr Sheat usually deals with murder cases, but he is on a three-week holiday in the Seychelles at the moment, so I'm afraid you've got me.'

'Three weeks in the Seychelles? And I always assumed you solicitors were hard up. It's not as if you charge a lot for your services.'

'You are welcome to find someone cheaper. But given what's at stake here it I wouldn't recommend it.'

'Okay. Where do we start?'

'Let's start from the beginning and tell me everything.'

'Ok. But my priority is to get out of here. Can you get me bail?'

'I can certainly apply for it. But it's not guaranteed. This is a murder case. It's very serious.'

'You don't say. I can see why they pay you the big bucks.'

'I would suggest you cooperate with me and not try to be clever. I am on your side, but you will have to help yourself too. It is not easy to get bail for a murder suspect. It can only be granted by a Crown Court judge. Perhaps it would be a good idea to tell me everything that has happened so far.'

Barney told him everything that had happened and Hadaway hummed and muttered at regular intervals. Barney wasn't overly impressed. But he had no choice but to go along with it.

'So what do you think?'

'Well my first impressions are that they don't seem to have all that much in the way of evidence. I think they might be wasting their time on you when the real culprit is still out there somewhere. But because it's such a high-profile case they have to be seen to be doing something. Police tend to get rather jumpy when they see themselves on the news. But let's just stay cool for the moment and see what their next move is. We'll see how their next round of questioning goes and take it from there. I'll be sitting in on any interviews from now on. But my advice would be to stop trying to be smart with them. You are not going to help yourself by winding them up.'

'But I enjoy it.'

'That may well be. But ease up on it if you want to get out of here soon.'

They were eventually joined in the interview room by Barlocks and Price. After the formalities and introductions, Barlocks started the questioning in a similar fashion to the previous day by waving a photograph in front of him.

'Do you recognise this man in the photograph?'

'Are we doing this again? My answer hasn't changed. As I told you before, he's a weasel faced flag shagger, who I didn't murder, but I can understand why someone would want to.'

'I think you need to look a little closer. This is not the same photograph that I showed you yesterday.'

Barney looked at the photograph. He had no idea who it was.

'No. I don't recognise him. Who is he?'

'He was arrested while hiding in your garden. Perhaps your wife knows him. Perhaps you need to focus on your own wife's extra curricular activities instead of worrying about mine.'

Hadaway intervened for the first time.

'Chief Inspector. That comment is wholly inappropriate. I must insist you concentrate on the matter in hand and refrain from insults and innuendo. Otherwise my client will not be obliged to answer your questions.'

'Very well. We shall concentrate on the matter in hand. And the matter in hand is this man in the photograph.'

'Did you say he was in my garden? What was he doing there?'

'I was hoping you could tell us.'

'How would I know. I've never seen him before in my life.'

'He seems to know a lot about you. Allow me to refresh your memory. His name is John Houskoller.'

Barney had heard the name before. But it took him a few moments to remember from where. Horace Horsecollar. Sue's partner. His expression visibly changed. Barlocks had a triumphant smirk.

'So you do know him then.'

'I know of someone with that name. A friend of a friend. But I've never met him. And I couldn't tell you if it's the same John Houskoller.'

'This particular John Houskoller was arrested last night while in the act of interfering with police evidence. He was hiding in the very spot where the body of Rupert Spiffington-Smythe was discovered.'

Hadaway intervened again.

'Chief Inspector. It has not yet been confirmed that it was the body of Rupert Spiffington-Smythe. As I understand it, you are still waiting for the final forensics report. I must insist that you avoid speculation and stick to actual facts.'

Barney was beginning to like this solicitor. Barlocks was a little aggrieved but continued.

'That may well be, but even if it wasn't Rupert Spiffington-Smythe, there was still someone murdered and buried there. And your client is the number one suspect.'

'I'm afraid that isn't how it works chief inspector. You have charged my client with the murder of Rupert Spiffington-Smythe. You can't just change the rules to suit yourself. And it now looks like you have a new suspect. That gets my client off the hook.'

'I'm afraid not. I am now working on the possibility that they were in it together. It's a lot easier for two people to carry dead bodies around.'

'Chief Inspector. As I said to my client before this interview, you don't appear to have much in the way of evidence. I therefore would request you drop the charges and release my client from custody.'

'Oh but that's where you're wrong. Some new evidence has come to light. Some quite compelling evidence I might add, and we certainly won't be dropping the charges.'

'Are you going to share this evidence with us?'

'No, not yet. Further investigations have to be conducted first. Mr Barnard. I would like you to confirm how long you have lived at your current address.'

'Seven years and two months.'

'Interesting.'

'Why is it interesting?'

'Because the experts are telling me that the body found in your garden was estimated to have died between five and eight years old. In other words, you were likely to have been living there when he was murdered.'

Hadaway pounced all over that.

'Chief Inspector. You are making an awful lot of assumptions on things which are yet to be proven. The body may or may not have been that of the person you are accusing my client of murdering. It might have been buried there while my client was living there. Or maybe not. You don't even know for sure that this was a murder. You are wasting your time. This will be thrown out of court.'

'You won't be saying that when you hear what the new evidence is that I have discovered.'

They were interrupted by another policeman who said something significant had come up regarding the case. Barlocks didn't enjoy the intervention. He told Price to go out and deal with it. Which he did, in a hurry. He could sense the bad mood overtaking Barlocks. He returned after five minutes.

'Sir, can I have a word outside?'

Barlocks reluctantly paused the interview recording and left the room with Price.

'We've been contacted by someone.'

'Yes. And?'

'This person is confessing to the murder of Rupert Spiffington-Smythe.'

28

Hadaway had left the police station, promising Barney he would try to get him out of there as soon as possible. Price and Barlocks turned their attention to the mysterious call they had received. Barlocks was sceptical about it.

'This caller didn't leave his name.'

'No sir. He said he was known as the Scorpion.'

'The Scorpion? He sounds like a crank. Somone who is winding us up.'

'On the face of it I agree. But there's something about it that is bugging me. I can't quite put my finger on it. But there's something familiar about the voice.'

'Let's hear it again then.'

They played the recording again.

'I am the Scorpion. It was me who murdered Rupert Spiffington-Smythe. But you'll never catch me. I'm too clever. I am far too clever. You'll never catch me. I am ke… I am the Scorpion.'

'He doesn't sound like a murderer to me. He just sounds like an annoying prat.'

'But the more I hear it, the more I think I've heard his voice before.'

'Keep thinking. Meanwhile let's have a chat with this Houskoller chap.'

Barney and Hadaway talked things over while they were left

alone. Hadaway sounded optimistic. He was confident he could win this case, but Barney wasn't so sure. He was concerned at what Barlocks had told them about some new compelling evidence. Hadaway tried to reassure him.

'I wouldn't worry too much about that. I've had to deal with policemen like him on many occasions. It's probably just bullshit.'

They were interrupted by a policewoman who escorted Barney back to his cell. Before Hadaway left he reminded him that he would like to get out of here. Hadaway promised he would do what he could.

Horace was brought to the interview room. He appeared to be timid and nervous. Much more to Barlocks's liking. He could put some pressure on him. Horace was a typical domestic abuser. He was a big man while bullying his girlfriend, checking her phone, telling her where she was allowed to go, who she was allowed to meet, what clothes she should wear. But underneath it all he was really just a snivelling coward when someone stood up to him.

'Right, Mr Housekoller. I have a few questions for you. And I want answers. Are we clear on that?'

'Er… yes… I er… yes.'

'Why were you at the house at which you were apprehended?'

'But… but I have already explained that to your colleagues.'

'I would like you to explain it all again to me. What were you doing at that house?'

'I discovered that my girlfriend was having an affair with someone called Barney. I found his address in her phone.'

'So you thought you'd go around there. And do what exactly?'

'I… I don't know. I just wanted to see him. I wasn't going to do anything. I hadn't really thought it through.'

'Do you have proof of this affair?'

'Yes. Well no. Not really.'

'You climbed over the garden fence. That is trespass at the very least. And there could be other charges. I am particularly interested in the location where you were found hiding.'

'What do you mean?'

'It was exactly the same spot where a murder victim was discovered. What do you know about that?'

Horace was horrified.

'Nothing. Nothing at all. I don't know anything about it.'

'What about Mr Barnard? How well do you know him?'

'I don't know him at all. I've never met him.'

'What did you intend doing to him when you met him.'

'I… er… I don't know. Nothing.'

Horace burst into tears. Barlocks had heard enough for now. He suspended the interview. Outside, Price and Barlocks discussed what they had just heard.

'What do you think sir?'

'I think he's a very good actor. I've come across the likes of him before. He doesn't fool me.'

Price said he agreed with him. Even though he didn't mean it. He didn't believe Horace had anything to do with the murder.

His mind was very much focussed on the Scorpion.

'Sir. Do you mind if we listen to that phone call again? I think I might be on to something.'

'Ok. But you need to start coming up with something very soon. I'm beginning to lose my patience with this case.'

They listened to it again.

'Play that bit at the very end again.'

They played it yet again.

'There. Did you hear it?'

'No.'

'Just before he says I am the Scorpion. It sound like he says I am Ke… He almost let slip his real name.'

They played it again.

'Oh yes. I see what you mean. Well spotted sergeant. But it still doesn't tell us much. What could the name be? Colin? Kevin? Keith? Ken? Carl? Callum?'

Then it started to fall into place for Price. He now knew where he had heard that voice before.

'Ken… Ken… Ken. But not Ken.'

'What are you on about?'

'How about Kenneth?'

29

Kenneth was sitting his flat feeling smug. He had given the police something to think about by confessing to the murder. He felt he could easily outsmart them, even though his track record didn't support this. He thought his plan to kidnap his former wife and make half a million quid was foolproof. But that didn't turn out well. It is difficult to understand what his motives were for his latest venture. He can't make any money out of it. His plan to stay anonymous had taken an unexpected twist with the involvement of Sergeant Price, who was the one who arrested him for the kidnapping. And the biggest twist of all is that even if he managed to convince everyone he was the murderer, the person who would benefit most would be Barney, the man he hated more than anyone. But he had no idea at this stage that the body had been discovered at the house of his ex wife and her husband.

Despite his bravado about being too smart to get caught, he subconsciously was hoping it would happen. He wanted to go back to prison. They were the happiest years of his life. He had taken the occasional beating, but he felt he was someone in there. The odds were that he would end up back inside either way. Even if they couldn't get him for murder, he would still be in trouble for breaching the terms of his parole.

He decided it was time to check out Facebook and see if there was anyone he could wind up.

He came across a thread which was titled British Comedy Classics and a clip from Love Thy Neighbour. These sorts of posts were regularly popping up and he was becoming bored with them. But he read the first few replies.

'Absolute classic. They don't make comedy like this no more.'

'I agree. It wouldn't be aloud. It would upset the woke brigade.

'i no there are too many snowflaks around these days the comidy these days is rubbish.'

'I agree. They are too many wokes around. You're not allowed to say anything no more…'

'I had a black fiend and he thought it was hilarias.'

'I meant frend.'

'I am black and was at school when this was on the telly. I didn't find anything hilarious about it. I was laughed at and called all kinds of racist words that the white kids had heard on this so-called comedy.'

Kenneth replied to this one.

'You need to develop a sense of humour.'

But he got no satisfaction from it. He realised it was a crap comment and deleted it straight away. There were no other posts that caught his attention, so he decided to start one of his own.

'Hello. I am the Scorpion.'

'Hello. I am a female scorpion. I like your photograph. Can we be friends? I will send you some photos. Message me.'

'I said I was the Scorpion, not a gullible moron. Get lost.'

Kenneth was about to give up and switch his laptop off when a few other people joined in.

'why are you the scorpion and are you reely a scorpion.'

'I am the Scorpion. I have murdered someone.'

'you shudent say such a thing not even jokeing muredering is not nice.'

'Who did you murder?'

'A former MP called Rupert Spiffington-Smythe.'

'Oh, I no him. I herd he was murdered.'

'Yes. That's what I'm trying to tell you. I murdered him.'

'i dont beleeve you murdered him.'

'Why not? You believe someone murdered him. So why not me?'

'becos if it really was you why would you come on here and tell people.'

Kenneth thought she had a point. This wasn't having the desired effect. He wasn't getting his usual twisted pleasure from the exchanges today. He logged out and turned off his laptop. Perhaps he would get a better response if he contacted the police again. They had a duty to take him seriously.

Meanwhile, back in the lake district two policemen were indeed taking him seriously.

'Kenneth? Who is Kenneth?'

'He was the one who did the kidnapping. I knew I recognised his voice from somewhere.'

'Are you sure?'

'Yes. Absolutely. I'd never forget him.'

'Interesting. And the body was found in the garden of the woman he kidnapped. This case is becoming more and more complicated. There is something funny going on and I'm struggling to put my finger on it. We now have three suspects.'

'Yes sir. But we don't have any strong evidence against any of them.'

'That's where you're wrong.'

'Oh yes. I've been meaning to ask you. You mentioned in the interview that you had some new evidence. Are you able to tell me what it is?'

'I'm still waiting for forensics to confirm something. Then I'll fill you in. Meanwhile, where would we find this Kenneth?'

'I assumed he would still be in prison. But I've just checked, and he was released on parole three weeks ago.'

'Where was he living before he went to prison?'

'Somewhere in Buckinghamshire. I can find out his exact address from his parole officer.'

'Buckinghamshire? That's a bit of a trek. But it's one we're going to have to make. Let's do it tomorrow. This case is doing my head in. Come on. Let's pop into the Dog and Trumpet. I could murder a pint.'

30

Brian Hadaway had done the job for Barney. He had managed to get him out on bail with the help of a Crown Court judge. He was relieved to be home, and wondered if he should perhaps have been a little more polite during the police interview. He wasn't aware of this yet, but Horace had also been released and had only been charged with trespassing. He would end up getting a fine and would no doubt take out his anger on Sue. Barlocks still had suspicions about him, but didn't have enough evidence yet to hold him. Nor was he aware that his old enemy Kenneth was now also a suspect.

He hadn't seen Alison since his return. She had taken Jack to school and then had gone to the doctors. It was for a routine medication review. She had been taking cocktail of tablets since her heart attack seven years ago. She also carried around a spray for emergency use. If she got any sudden pains in her chest she needed to spray it under her tongue. She had only used it on two occasions. Once when she thought she felt pain but on reflection was probably imagining it. The other time when she was drunk in the pub and was demonstrating it to her friends. She wasn't expecting anything bad but was always nervous on her visits to the doctors. The doctor doing the review was a woman in her thirties and was very friendly and reassuring. They chatted for a while about how she was feeling in general. Just the usual questions. Whether she had experienced any pain, or breathlessness, dizziness etc. She took her blood pressure reading and took a blood sample. Then she delivered her analysis.

Barney hadn't had much sleep lately stuck in that police cell and would have liked to lie down for a couple of hours. But that wasn't to be. He had a phone call from the school. Much to his dismay, it was Mrs Solly.

'Mr Barnard. Jack is not having a good day. He is being very disruptive in class. Would you please come and take him home?'

'I am about 70 miles away at the moment. Have you tried calling Mrs Barnard?'

'Yes, but she isn't answering. You will need to come at once.'

'I can come, but like I said, I am 70 miles away. If the traffic is as bad as it usually is. it could take me at least an hour, or maybe two.'

'Very well. Just get here as soon as possible.'

Barney ended the call, rolled over and attempted to fall asleep. But he couldn't. He was too restless now. He tossed and turned for an hour, then got in the car and headed for the school. Once there he was taken to Mrs Solly's office. A room he was all too familiar with.

'I'm afraid Jack has been very disruptive this morning. He has been shouting in class and throwing objects at the other children.'

'I see. Where is he now?'

'He's still in the classroom.'

'Is he still being disruptive?'

'No. He has calmed down now.'

'So there isn't any need to take him home.'

'I'm afraid you must. We have a procedure we must adhere to.'

'Then your procedure is barmy.'

'Whether you think it's barmy is neither here nor there. You must follow our instructions.'

'When I was at school we had kids with autism and ADHD and such. They didn't have those labels for them, but I assume they still existed. Such kids were just treated as naughty children and were dealt with it appropriately. The schools didn't ring the parents every ten minutes expecting parents to just walk out of their jobs at the drop of a hat. They dealt with it. I think it's about time you tried doing the same instead of sitting around scratching your arse all day. The only solution you seem to have for kids with what you label 'special educational needs' is to ship them off to another school and let them deal with the problem. So how does that help the children? For your information, it doesn't. So I'm going back home. I'm not taking him out of school when he's behaving perfectly well.'

'Mr Barnard. I must insist…

'Put a sock in it. I'm not listening. I've had enough of your relentless whining. And don't call me again unless you've got something positive to say. Goodbye.'

On that note he walked out. When he arrived home Alison was already back. She didn't look happy. On the contrary, she looked very unhappy. Barney feared the worst. He walked towards her. He attempted to hug her but the look on her face told him not to.

'What did the doctor say? Did it not go well?'

'No. It was fine. No dramas there. I'm perfectly healthy.'

'That's a relief. I got the feeling they'd given you some bad news. Looking at your demeanour.'

'Yes. I have received some bad news. But not from the doctors. I've just had a call from the school. They have told me all about your verbal attack on Mrs Solly. They are saying we will have to find a different school for Jack to go to. They don't want him there any longer thanks to you.'

'Good. Let's find one that is where they are willing to teach him and make some effort to understand him instead of finding fault with him all the time.'

'Why do you have to be so confrontational?'

'I'm sticking up for our son, and I think you ought to be doing the same.'

Alison stormed out of the room and slammed the door. Barney switched the television on but wasn't taking any notice of it. Ten minutes later Alison returned, and her mood hadn't improved.

'And another thing. I don't appreciate being left here on my own while some madman breaks into our garden.'

'I didn't leave you. I was arrested. I had no say in the matter.'

Yes. You were arrested. You don't see me getting arrested.'

'I didn't have a choice in the matter. What did you expect me to do? Sorry officer, I must decline your arrest. I don't really fancy being arrested today. Maybe come back tomorrow? Or can we just forget the whole thing? Thank you officer.'

'Do you realise how horrible it was knowing there was

someone out there creeping around watching me?'

'It must have been awful for you. Meanwhile I was having a right old laugh locked up in a cell all night.'

Alison went out again and slammed the door even harder. He wondered how that door was still intact. She went off to the school to bring Jack home.

31

The following day Barney received a phone call from his friend Neil, who was unexpectedly in the area because of a case he was working on.

'I shall be staying around until tomorrow afternoon. Would you like to go out for a few beers tonight.'

'Yes. I wouldn't say no. Do you want to stay over at our place?'

'No, I wouldn't like to impose. I've already got a hotel. Have you any suggestions where we could go?'

'There's a pub called the Oddfellows Arms which is not too far from our house. It's the only one around here that's got a dartboard. And they'll have the football on TV. I don't know what the food is like, but we can give it a try.'

'Sounds good to me. I should be knocking off at about five, so I'll nip back to the hotel for a shower and change then I'll head over.'

They met at around 6.30 and played darts until 8.00. Then they sat down to watch the football and have some food. They spent half an hour debating the problems of Sunderland and whether the manager should be sacked. Like most football fans they thought they could do a better job than their manager. Then Barney told Neil all about being arrested for murder, and everything else that had been going on.

'Bloody hell! You don't half get yourself into some situations. First it's punch ups with loan sharks. Then it's kidnapping.

Now it's murder. Trouble just seems to follow you around. This one has been all over the news. Do they seriously think this missing MP has been found in your garden? And that you might have killed him? That's mindboggling.'

'I know. I don't suppose you have any professional advice to offer me? I'm worried about this new evidence which apparently been discovered.'

'Not really. But this supposed new evidence could be something or nothing. Your solicitor doesn't think it is anything to be concerned about.'

'That's true. But I don't trust solicitors. I think they just want to get rich.'

'That's not the way you should be thinking. You definitely needed a solicitor, and you did the right thing in getting one. I just hope he knows his stuff.'

'He came across as knowing his stuff. He had some clever answers that tied Inspector Bollocks in knots. And he did manage to secure my release.'

'There you go then. I know some of them are rubbish, but most of them know what they are doing. I get to know a lot of solicitors in my line of work. What is their name?'

'Hadaway and Sheat.'

'Yes. I do know them. They are one of the better ones.'

'So other than telling me I've got a good solicitor that's taking all my money off me, do you have any other advice?'

'I doubt it. I don't usually investigate murders. People hire me to follow their wives to see if they are having an affair or to trace a person who has disappeared. But not high-profile MPs.

It sounds as if they don't have much on you. Just be patient. I would have thought… I'm not boring you am I? Your mind seems to be elsewhere.'

'Yes. Sorry. That man who just walked in. I think I recognise him.'

'Who is he?'

'Horace Horsecollar.'

Neil laughed.

'Not his real name I assume?'

'No. He's the one who was creeping around our garden when I was locked up.'

'You'd better not let him see you then. From what you told me he's really got it in for you for messing around with his girlfriend.'

'I haven't been messing around with his girlfriend. We just went for a drink, that's all.'

'Oh yes. The number of times I have heard that.'

'Bollocks! Anyway, it wouldn't matter if he did see me. I've never met him. He doesn't know what I look like. I only know him from a photograph the police showed me.'

'He looks a bit of a creep to me. I meet his sort all the time in my line of work. Jealous husbands who are convinced their wives are having affairs and hire me to follow them, only to find out they have been secretly going to keep fit classes or taking horse riding lessons. It's easy money really.'

'What case are you working on at the moment?'

'A woman in Durham wants me to find her son that went missing. I got a lead that brought me here. I've got high hopes of finding him tomorrow.'

'That's awful. I hope you find him. I know I complain about Jack, but I would be devastated if he went missing. How old is this boy you're looking for?'

'63.'

'You daft bugger. I thought you were talking about a little kid. How long has he been missing?'

'27 years.'

Barney shook his head in disbelief.

'You'd better hurry then. I've heard it gets difficult to find them once they've been missing for 30 years.'

Neil laughed.

'I'll go and get the beers in.'

Even though he was sure Horace wouldn't recognise him, Barney felt nervous. He wasn't aware Horace was an abject coward and would probably run a mile if Barney went over and introduced himself. Thankfully he only stayed for two pints without talking to anyone, then quietly left. Barney and Neil had their food which turned out to be of decent quality and plenty more drinks, then Neil called for a taxi to take him back to the hotel. As usual Barney was too mean to pay for a taxi and set off walking home.

Four days passed quietly by without further incident. They were looking at alternative schools for Jack, but his school hadn't been putting on any extra pressure for him to leave. They had discovered that it wasn't quite so easy for a school to exclude a pupil. Barney was now very keen to move him to a different school. Alison would prefer to leave him where he is. She had visited Mrs Solly and attempted to undo the damage Barney had done. If it turned out that Jack was allowed to stay there, he wasn't going to argue, so long as it was Alison that went to deal with the problems next time one of them was summoned. He just wanted a quiet life.

He was getting a quiet life today at least. It was Saturday, and a bit of normality had returned. Alison had gone out shopping. She wanted some new shoes, so would be gone for a few hours. Barney had plenty of sport to watch on the television. He had a decent supply of beer in the fridge. Jack was playing loudly with his train set but was absorbed with it enough to leave him alone apart from the occasional daft question. The cats were both asleep. George was on the sofa next to him. Mildred was curled up under the table. The police hadn't bothered him for a few days. He had tried to put the murder case out of his mind, but it wasn't easy. He had no idea what would happen next. It was such a bizarre situation. He was briefly interrupted by Jack flinging one of his train carriages across the room because it was annoying him for some reason. But he was soon placated, and Barney got back to his television. There was a break in the sport for a news update. He didn't mind. It was a chance to catch up on what was going on in the world. A chance to rant at the inept politicians that were supposedly running the country. But he didn't get the chance to rant. He was rendered speechless by the astonishing images that appeared on the screen. He got to his feet and accidentally kicked his drink over, but he never noticed. He was just staring in disbelief at what he was seeing on the television.

32

The same images were on display on the screen in the Dog and Trumpet, but nobody was watching it. The sound was turned down and music was blaring out instead. It was the sort of pub where the only thing anyone watched on the television was sport. It would have been more appealing to the punters if Sky sports news was on. But instead, there was a news channel on and various politicians waffling away about something boring and irrelevant.

Barlocks and Price certainly weren't taking any notice of it. Price had reluctantly accepted Barlocks's invitation to have a drink. In reality he didn't have a lot of choice. It was Saturday and he had other things he needed to be getting on with. But Barlocks told him he had something very important to tell him, and it couldn't wait.

'Thanks for coming Sergeant. But I just had to tell you this today so we can get things moving along as soon as possible.'

'That's ok sir. I wasn't planning on doing much else today.'

Price had to lie. He had plenty of things he was planning on doing today. One of them was to go out to lunch with the mother of one of the main suspects in the case. Barlocks sounded so excited when he called Price to tell him he wanted to meet him. Price wasn't sharing the excitement. He was now filled with apprehension.'

'That's good. Because I believe I have cracked the case.'

'You know who the murderer is?'

'Yes. I have finally got hold of the evidence I have been waiting for.'

'That's excellent news. Who is it?'

'No. Let's do this properly. Round up the suspects.'

'With all due respect sir, that isn't doing it properly. That might be how they do it on Death in Paradise. But it doesn't happen that way in real life.'

'Why not?'

'For a start, we can't make the suspects come. Kenneth would have to travel from Buckinghamshire. He may be a bit of an oddball, but it's unlikely he would want to do that. From our dealings with Houskoller I would guess he is probably too afraid to come out of his house. And I'm fairly certain Barnard would tell us to take a hike.'

Barlocks sighed and realised Price was right. But he still had the satisfaction of solving the murder. And because it was such a high-profile case, he was going to be famous.

'Are you going to tell me who the murderer is?'

'Ok. You'll be pleased to know that it's almost certainly Cecil Barnard, aided and abetted by John Houskoller. It's pretty conclusive evidence. I'm going to be famous. Er… I mean we are going to be famous.'

Price didn't react in the manner he was anticipating.

'Oh.'

'Oh? Oh? Is that all you've got to say? I thought you would be happy about that. I thought you were determined to nick this joker.'

'I may have been last week. But my circumstances have changed. In fact I think I will have to be taken off the case altogether.'

'Whatever for? This could be the greatest moments of our careers. I'm more than happy to take all the credit if you're not bothered.'

'I think you would call it a conflict of interest.'

'What on earth are you talking about?'

Price didn't hear the question. His attention had wandered elsewhere.

'Sergeant. Am I boring you?'

Price didn't answer. He was staring at the television.

Barlocks looked up and saw the face of Rupert Spiffington-Smythe on the screen.

'Why are you looking so surprised? He's been in the news a lot lately. And soon he's going to be in the news a lot more when we've successfully prosecuted his murderer.'

'I don't think that is very likely sir.'

'It's more than likely. I'm telling you this is nailed on.'

'Have a closer look. Look at that caption on the bottom left. It says 'Live'.'

'What are you getting at?'

'What I'm getting at is, the man whose murder you have just claimed to have solved is getting interviewed on television at this very moment.'

33

Kenneth had expected to get caught. That's what he really wanted. But he never expected it to happen so quickly. It was his own fault. He had inadvertently let slip his real name when he called the police. Now they were coming for him. A top cop from Manchester, along with the prat who arrested him for the kidnapping. Normally the police would turn up unannounced in a case like this, but they had no intention of driving all the way to Buckinghamshire only to find he'd gone out. They never told him they were going to arrest him for murder, but he wasn't stupid. He knew what was going to happen. Or at least he thought he did. He hadn't seen the news. He wanted to have one last moment of glory on social media before he was taken away. He logged into Facebook.

'This is the Scorpion. This is the last time you will hear from me. This afternoon I will be taken away and incarcerated for the murder of Rupert Spiffington-Smythe.'

'I think UR crazy.'

'You're right. I am crazy. You have to be crazy to be a murderer.'

'no I mean u have to b crazy to think u murdered him. He issent even dead.'

'ees right he isnt ded. I saw him on TV this morning.'

'What are you talking about? He is dead. I killed him myself.'

'he is rite nd not only if that is and still alive olso.'

'In Inglish please?'

'hear come the grammer pollice agane.'

'Ok, tell me this. If he isn't dead, where has he been for the last seven years?'

'In a monessterry on an iland in the outer hebradees living with some munks.'

'Yes. He found god.'

'No. That can't be. I killed him, I killed him, I killed him.'

'Ha ha you diddent do a very good job of it. unless he said a prair to god and got brought back from the dead.'

'Liar! Liar!' He's dead!'

Kenneth kicked the table leg in anger and then screeched in agony because he forgot he wasn't wearing any shoes. Once the pain had subsided, he logged out of Facebook. He needed to find out if there was any truth in what they were saying. He frantically hammered away at the keyboard while simultaneously turning the television on. But before he could find out what he needed to know, he was interrupted by the sound of the doorbell. This got him excited. Nobody ever visited him, so the police must be here after all. He opened the door, and his excitement was replaced by disappointment. It was his probation officer. He had come to inform him that calling the police and pretending to be a murderer, even if the alleged victim was still alive, was a breach of his probation conditions. He would be getting his wish of going back to prison after all.

34

Alison and Barney were sitting in their garden relaxing and sharing a bottle of wine. They were feeling relieved that the ridiculous murder business was over. They both agreed they could do with a quiet spell in their lives and concentrate their efforts on Jack. His school problems need to be sorted. What with the kidnapping and murder, they had never been able to give him full attention he required. It was time to get back to normal. Maybe take another holiday. Then Barney made an announcement which took Alison by surprise.

'I've decided to use the glider flight we won at the school raffle.'

'Are you sure? I thought you were terrified at the thought of it.'

'I'm not terrified. I'm just not keen on being high up.'

'I've got news for you mate. A glider is going to be high up.'

'Alright, alright. Don't put me off. I'm going to call them now and book myself in.'

Barney dug out the voucher which had been thrown in a drawer and had just been lying there forgotten about. But clearly not completely forgotten. He picked up his phone and dialled the number on the voucher. He got through to an airfield which was seventeen miles from where they lived. After a ten-minute call during which he was asked a few questions, he ended the call. He sat in silence for a while. Alison was getting impatient.

'Well?'

'They can fit me in tomorrow afternoon. After we pick up Jack from school.'

'Are you going to do it?'

'I suppose so.'

'You don't sound as keen as you did ten minutes ago.'

'No. I am still keen. Let's do it.'

Alison was amazed that he was even considering going through with it. She had witnessed his legs turning to jelly on the tower of Durham Cathedral. She had seen him trembling with fear on ski lifts, and she had watched him chicken out of the fairground rides at Blackpool Pleasure Beach. Therefore she had doubts that he would go up in the glider. She guessed the reason he was contemplating doing it was that he was such a stubborn sod that it was his prize and nobody else was going to have it. He was going to use it even if it frightened him to death. There was some truth in that, but it was more that he wanted to overcome his fear and prove something to himself.

The following day they both collected Jack from the school and drove straight to the airfield. Jack was very excited by it all and was babbling away about how high the gliders went and how dangerous it was. This wasn't doing anything to help Barney. He was unusually quiet, and Alison could sense he was nervous to put it mildly.

'If you don't think you can handle it, there's nothing wrong with changing your mind even at the last minute. I won't tell anyone.'

'I'm not going to change my mind. I'm doing it.'

They arrived at the reception, and he handed the voucher to the lady sitting behind the desk.

'Good afternoon. Ah, this is the voucher I donated to the school raffle. Now I remember you.'

'What do you mean?'

'I was there when you won it. My son is Jamie Cummins. I believe he is in the same class as your son. I take it this little chap is Jack?'

'Yes, it is. I've not seen you at the school gates.'

'No. I'm usually working here most afternoons, so my husband picks up Jamie. I hope you have a good flight. It's a lovely day for it. You should get a fantastic view from miles up in the sky.'

She introduced them to a pilot who drove them out in a jeep to the spot where a glider and an aeroplane were parked. They got out of the jeep and Barney stared at the glider. It was Alison's turn to look worried.

'What's wrong?'

'I can't go through with it. Let's go back.'

'No, you can't. It's too late to back down now.'

'But only a half an hour ago you said it would be ok for me to cry off at the last minute.'

'That was before I knew one of the people who worked here had a son in the same class as Jack.'

'What's that got to do with anything?'

'If she tells her son and it get around the school that his dad chickened out, he would be the laughing stock of the school. It wouldn't be very nice for him.'

'It wouldn't be very nice for me to go up in this flimsy looking contraption that looks like it could fall apart at any moment just to save Jack from a bit of teasing at school.'

'Just get on with it.'

'The schoolkids don't need to find out. I'll just have a word with Mrs Cummins and tell her to keep it quiet.'

At this point Jack put paid to that idea.

'Daddy. Are you too scared to go in the glider?'

'Terrific. There's no chance of keeping it secret now.'

'Look. Just do it or I'll tell Mary and Liam.'

'What have they got to do with it?

'You took the piss out of Mary on that flight to Sharm El Sheikh when she got scared. I think they would enjoy getting their revenge when they hear what a coward you are.'

That remark angered Barney, and he stormed over towards the glider.

'I am not a coward!'

Alison smiled. She knew how to pull his strings. Barney approached the pilot.

'Ok mate. I'm ready when you are.'

'Great. Climb into the front seat and I'll be sitting behind you. I'll fasten your straps for you and run through a few safety checks and we'll soon be on our way.'

'Safety checks. What do you mean safety checks?'

'Don't worry. The checks are just part of the procedure we must follow before every launch. Just relax and enjoy it. You're perfectly safe.'

'Yeah right. Just relax he says.'

They completed the safety checks, and the glider was attached to the tow cable on the plane by one of the ground crew. The plane pilot revved its engine, and the glider lurched forward. There was no going back now. As both aircraft picked up speed it was somewhat scary, but once they had left the ground, he found it rather exhilarating. Once they were high up in the air the pilot released the tow cable and the plane flew off. Then it became almost silent. The only sound was the wind. The pilot flew the glider through a few gentle manoeuvres at first. Barney was beginning to enjoy it.

'Would you like to take the controls for a while?'

'What? Are you sure? Is that normal?'

'Yes. Don't worry. Nothing can go wrong. I still have my controls in the back if anything happens.'

Barney took hold of the joystick and put his feet on the pedals. He soon got the hang of it and flew in a straight line for a while. Then the pilot encouraged him to turn the glider around. So he did. He did a few circles and put it into a dive so it would speed up. After Barney had his moment of glory, the pilot took back control and did some showing off. He did a loop the loop, and put it into a spin so it hurtled towards the ground. Barney wasn't so keen on that bit, but the pilot levelled it out in time to execute a perfect landing. He put it down on the airfield with a gentle bump, and Barney felt a huge sense of relief.

Soon he was reunited with his family. Alison kissed him.

'How was it?'

'Fuc… Er… flipping brilliant!'

Jack, for a change didn't pick up on the almost swear word.

'Well done daddy. I will tell everybody at school you flew the glider.'

That comment pleased Barney. Jack very rarely said anything nice to him. It made a change to do something his son could be proud of. Alison was pleased too.

'How are you feeling after that?'

'I could murder a pint.'

'In that case we had better go and find you one.'

35

It was seven weeks since Rupert Spiffington-Smythe emerged from his self-imposed exile. Life had slowly returned to normal. Chief Inspector Barlocks had returned to Manchester. Kenneth was back in prison. The school had stopped calling to complain about Jack. Amazingly Barney's rant had deterred Mrs Solly from calling him. And the planned darts match between Barney's team the Mickey Mouse Club and Sue's team the Odd Fellows was finally going to happen.

There was a good turnout of the Mickey mouse club as there always was for their annual match on tour. There was Roy, the team captain whose main reason for being there was to try the beer in some pubs he'd never been in before. Then there was Fiona, the best player in the team and she had brought along her wife Marie. Tom had brought his girlfriend Cheryl, which was a surprise to the others as nobody expected their relationship to last this long, especially as he had already spent his share of the money, mainly on her. The cynics in the team, i.e. all of them were convinced she was only after his money and would be gone as soon as the money was. Yet here she was. And of course there was Daffy, the joker in the pack. Mary and Liam also made the trip even though they weren't into darts, but they didn't want to miss out on the fun. It was the autumn half term break and they were going to spend a few days here and make it a mini holiday. There was plenty to amuse the kids, and they might even squeeze in a day trip Blackpool. Barney had driven Jack and Louis to his mum's house early on Saturday morning so that Alison could also come along to the darts. It wasn't the first time Elizabeth had looked after them both. She liked them and they liked her. Her strategy for keeping them happy was a simple one. Load them up with as many sweets and crisps as they could eat, let them watch cartoons on the telly, and wait until they were exhausted before putting them to bed. Alison had protested previously at her approach to babysitting, but Elizabeth was stubborn and was going to do it her way. If they didn't like it they could pay for a childminder, which Alison would happily do but Barney was having none of it. The downside was that they would have to drive back to collect him on Sunday morning and would be expected to stay to dinner with the inevitable horrible hangovers.

Barney hurried back. He knew the gang would be starting early and didn't want to miss anything. They all congregated in the local pub, and it gave Mary the chance to resume the verbal battle she usually had in her love/hate relationship she had with Daffy.

'Well, well. If it isn't Daffius the Orgasm Giver. How are you doing? Do you still think you're the funniest person on earth?'

'Of course. So if you don't want your sides to split you'd better put in some earplugs. And how are you Sweary Mary?'

'Fucking great.'

'Oh how I've missed you.'

'Bollocks.'

'And I see you've widened your vocabulary range.'

The conversation continued like this while the others talked to each other in a more civilised manner. But the drinks flowed as they visited as many pubs as they could squeeze into the day, and by the time they arrived at the Oddfellows Arms for the darts they were already well oiled. The Odd Fellows were already in the pub when they arrived and were throwing darts at the board, looking like they meant business. The Mickey Mouse club hoped this lot weren't taking the game too seriously. They enjoyed a competitive game, but didn't want to get a hammering.

The Mickey Mouse Club were invited to have a warm up and started throwing a few practice darts. Just as Daffy was halfway through a throw, a door opened next to the board and a man stepped out. It appeared to be an entrance to the cellar. The scoreboard was hanging on the door, and they never even realised it was a door until it opened. Throughout the game there were frequent interruptions with staff going into the cellar. It didn't matter so much when they entered, but it was most inconvenient when they exited unexpectedly and one of the players was in mid throw. It didn't really matter too much on this occasion as it was just a friendly, but the Mickey Mouse Club could only imagine the arguments this would cause with some of the teams in their league in London, particularly Johnson and Smith, the most miserable team in the league. They would complain about the light being too bright, or not bright enough, their opponents talking too loudly while they were throwing, the wobbly floorboard, or even the quality of the sandwiches. If they had to play in this place with the door behind the scoreboard they would have walked out in disgust.

Following long winded introductions, the darts eventually got underway and after the first few games it seemed that the two teams were evenly matched. Barney won his pairs game teamed up with Daffy and then had the chance to chat to Sue, who had also had a few drinks before she had arrived. He was relieved she hadn't brought Horace along. That could have been uncomfortable for Alison, coming face to face with the man who has caused her such a fright a few weeks back.

'How's it going Sue?'

'Terrific.'

'How's Horace been treating you?'

'He's gone. I took your advice. I finally got the courage to throw him out. I realised he was no good for me.'

'To be fair I didn't actually advise you to leave him. I just asked why you stayed with him. But having said that, I think you did the right thing. What happens now? Do you get to keep the house?'

'Yes. It was mine in the first place. You must come around some time. I'm a single woman these days.'

There was a suggestive tone in her voice which made Barney uncomfortable.

'I'm not though. Single man I mean.'

'That's a shame.'

Sue glanced across at Alison, and Alison looked back briefly before turning away. The game continued, as did the consumption of drinks. The match had reached the halfway point, and the Odd Fellows were leading 5-3. Sue wandered back to Barney again and by now she was very drunk. She got very close to him and started getting touchy feely.

'Hi Barney darling.'

'Erm. Hi.'

'Don't be so uncomfortable. Surely you must know how I feel about you?'

'I, er, I… I'm.'

'I love you.'

Alison had been keeping an eye on things and wandered over.

'Am I interrupting anything?'

Barney thought for a moment. Then he burst out laughing.

'Oh my god. I don't believe you're trying that again. Do you seriously think I'm dumb enough to fall for the same prank?'

'It's not a prank. I've never met this woman before.'

'Don't you dare refer to me as this woman.'

But Barney wasn't falling for it this time.

'Yawn.'

'I'm telling you; this is not a prank.'

'Yawn, yawn.'

Sue intervened.

'Why do you put up with this bitch? You're far too good for her.'

That was the final straw for Alison. She swung a punch as hard as she could and caught Sue squarely on the jaw, and she fell to the floor. One of the Odd Fellows retaliated by violently shoving Alison who fell backwards and knocked over Marie who landed on the floor and started crying. This angered Fiona. Nobody was going to get away with making her wife cry. She picked up a chair and swung it at the head of the man who had just pushed Alison. But he ducked out of the way and the chair smashed into a table resulting in broken glass and drinks flying everywhere. This resulted in a mass brawl and complete chaos. The Odd Fellows would have had the edge in terms of numbers and physical strength, but the Mickey Mouse Club had their secret weapon in the shape of Liam whose karate skills laid out three of their team.

Meanwhile the staff had called the police, and they promptly arrive to a scene of utter chaos and destruction. They calmed everyone down and asked witnesses what had taken place. The witnesses all were clear about one thing. It was Alison who had thrown the first punch. Therefore, she was the first one who they handcuffed. Barney tried not to laugh. He remembered her exact words a few weeks ago. 'You were arrested. You don't see me getting arrested.'

The police took Alison out of the pub, and also arrested Fiona, which prompted Marie to burst into tears again. The Odd Fellows had all left the pub, apart from Sue who was receiving some medical treatment from a first aid expert. Daffy surveyed the wreckage around the room. He turned to Roy.

'I suppose this means we are not going to finish the darts match?'

'No. I wouldn't have thought so. But it doesn't matter. It was just a friendly after all.'

Barney was in a state of shock. He had wrongly assumed he was being pranked and he had seen his wife assault someone and start a riot, then get arrested. He had received a whack in the eye which would probably look horrible in the morning. But he had escaped reasonably lightly. In truth he was a bit of a wimp when it came to fighting, so his involvement had been as minimal as he could get away with. He saw Sue getting the first aid treatment and wandered over to her.

'Are you okay?'

'Not really. Thanks to your wife.'

'Don't worry. She's getting her comeuppance for it now. And to be fair not only did you insult her, but you were coming on strong with her husband.'

'I suppose so.'

'What will you do now? Do you need to go to the hospital?'

'No. I'm going home. I don't suppose you want to come with me? Now that your wife is otherwise occupied.'

'You never give up do you? Look, I would have loved to have got together with you all those years back when I was single. But I'm married now, and my wife is spending the night in a cell. What sort of person would I be if I cheated on her in those circumstances? Or any circumstances for that matter. You don't want to hook up with another ratbag. You've only just got rid of the last one. You need to find a better class of boyfriend. Or have a spell without one.'

'You're probably right. And I'm sorry about Alison.'

'That's ok. In fact I think it's quite funny. And it is a big boost for a man's ego having women fighting over him. It's the first time it's happened to me as far as I know. Apart from the one that genuinely was a prank.'

'Goodbye Barney. I might see you around. And if ever you want another friendly darts match, just feel free to pick up the phone and call somebody else.'

He laughed, then leaned forward and kissed her on the cheek.

'Ow! That fucking hurt!'

'Oops. Sorry.'

36

Barney woke up on Sunday morning with a monster hangover and the added pain of a sore eye. When he stumbled to the bathroom to relieve his bursting bladder, he caught a glimpse of himself in the mirror and saw the huge black eye. He would dearly love to go back to bed and stay there all day. Dinner at his mum's house had even less appeal than usual. But he had to collect Jack and Louis, so there was no way of getting out of it. Alison hadn't returned yet so it was looking as though he would have to go on his own. He waited as late as he dared, but an hour before noon he decided she wasn't being released yet so he got in the car and set off. It was a tough journey. The beautiful scenery didn't have the same charm when he was in this condition. It took him longer than usual too. When he arrived, he found there was another guest coming to dinner. He couldn't resist using one of the guest's catchphrases.

'Well, well, well. Who have we got here then? If it isn't Sergeant Prick.'

'Cecil! Don't be so rude. That is no way to talk to a guest in my house. Where is Alison? And what the heck has happened to your face?'

'I'm afraid Alison won't be joining us today. She has been otherwise detained.'

'Why? Has something happened?'

'Yes. That's one way of putting it.'

'Are you going to stop messing about and tell me what has happened?'

'She punched someone in the face last night in the pub. She was arrested and taken to the police station where she spent the night in a cell.'

'You shouldn't make jokes like that. I don't find it funny. Where is she really?'

'It's true I'm afraid. She is probably going to get charged with assault and actual bodily harm. I'm no expert on the exact terminology. Perhaps our top cop here could enlighten us.'

Price stayed silent.

'Or maybe he's more concerned with arresting innocent citizens for murdering someone who is still alive.'

The last thing Price wanted to talk about was the murder so then he chipped in about the events of yesterday.

'Yes, it is true. There was a barney in the Oddfellows arms last night. The police were in attendance and two arrests were made.'

'You mean this Barney?'

'No, not Barney. A barney.'

'I have no idea what you are talking about. What's a barney?'

'A fight.'

'Why's it called a barney?'

'I don't know.'

Barney decided to enlighten them.

'If you look it up on Google it says, 'angry argument, altercation, row'.'

'In that case it's very appropriate to be named after my son.'

'It isn't named after me. It's cockney rhyming slang. Barney Rubble. He's Fred Flintstone's neighbour. Barney Rubble? Trouble?'

'I see. But his wife is called Betty Rubble. They could have just as easily called it a betty.'

'It doesn't sound quite the same. There was a bit of a betty down the pub last night. However, their son is called Bamm-Bamm.' That sounds better. There was a bit of a Bamm-Bamm down the pub last night.'

Once this ridiculous conversation had come to an end, there was a long spell of silence from all of them. Elizabeth was in the kitchen putting the final touches to the dinner. Barney and Price sat uncomfortably in the lounge. Barney pretended to be interested in Jack and asked him all kinds of pointless questions, just to avoid talking to Price. But once they had sat down at the kitchen table, he couldn't resist asking the question.

'What brings you here? I thought you two had fallen out?'

Elizabeth answered first.

'No. We are very much friends again. Even more than friends. I have something to tell you. I would have liked to tell you and Alison together, but I suppose she will have to wait. The sergeant and I are getting married.'

'Wow! I wasn't expecting that. That's a turn up for the books. When is it going to happen?'

'We haven't set a date yet. But it will be sometime in the Spring.'

'Congratulations.'

'You don't have to go overboard with excitement.'

'Sorry. It's not that I'm not happy for you. It's just that I'm very hung over, my wife is a hooligan who has just spent the night in the nick, and I've just found out Dixon of Dock Green here is going to be my new stepdad.'

Neither of them answered him. Elizabeth dished out the food and asked Price if he would like to say Grace. But Barney stepped in.

'Let me say Grace today.'

Price said it was fine by him. But Elizabeth wasn't so keen.

'Don't encourage him. He'll just say something silly and rude.'

'No I won't. I promise I will be serious and sincere.'

Elizabeth reluctantly agreed. They put their hands together and closed their eyes. Barney put on the most serious voice he could muster.

'Dear god. I am led to believe we owe you thanks as it is you that provides us with this food. It's not that I'm ungrateful or anything, but there are millions of people in the world including many children who are starving to death. If it is indeed your job to feed us, why are you letting this happen? You must be a very cruel, or some might even say evil god. I am not a selfish person, so all I can say is thanks for nothing. Amen.'

Elizabeth and Price didn't add their usual 'amen'. Elizabeth scowled and was thinking of the best way to respond. Price didn't look all that happy either. They lived in a bubble where criticism of God was not the done thing. But Barney had taken the moral high ground, and for all their strong beliefs, they had no real answer to him. He didn't feel he had been unnecessarily rude, and hopefully he had given them something to think about. Elizabeth finally spoke.

'There is no need to be so disrespectful. Just because you don't believe in something doesn't give you the right to ridicule those of us that do.'

'I wasn't ridiculing you. On the contrary, I was raising a valid point. Do you blindly believe your god is all good, or do you ever question some of the things he does? For instance, what about that seven-year-old girl that was hit by that drunk driver last month, not too far from here. She lay in the hospital in an intensive care unit for three days before she died. You and your fellow god botherers were saying prayers for her every day and encouraging others to do the same.'

'What's so wrong with that?'

'Are you telling me God had the power to save her, but would only do it if enough people begged him to do it? Then he ignored everyone and let her die anyway.'

'He moves in mysterious ways. He has reasons for everything he does.'

'In that case what was the point in saying the prayers if he was just going to do what he wanted anyway?'

Price butted in.

'I've seen some horrific things in my time as a policeman. I've sometimes questioned my own belief in God. I once went to the vicar and asked him why God allowed so many horrible things to happen. He told me we were all God's children and was allowing the human race to learn from its mistakes. Put it this way. If your son fell off his bike, you wouldn't take his bike off him. You would encourage him to get back on it and just try not to fall off it next time.'

'Yes, I would. But if he was mugging old ladies at knifepoint to fund a heroin addiction, I would step in and do anything that was necessary to stop him. And I think my example is a much more accurate reflection of human 'mistakes' than your one.'

'I see. Are you suggesting God should take a more hands on approach?'

'No. I'm suggesting God doesn't exist. My argument is a purely hypothetical one. I wanted to give you something to think about. Saying grace is a selfish act. I'm alright God. Thanks for the grub. Sod everyone else.'

Jack then made a surprising contribution to the conversation.

'Thanks Grandma for this food.'

Barney was proud of him. It took a six-year-old to make the most sensible comment of the day.

'I would also like to say thanks mum for cooking us dinner.'

Elizabeth didn't know how to answer. She was in a state somewhere between pride and irritation.

At this point the conversation came to an end, much to everyone's relief, and they started to eat their food.

During dinner Barney asked Price how Barlocks had responded to finding out Rupert Spiffington-Smythe was alive all along. Price explained that Barlocks didn't let anyone know about his claim to have evidence that solved the murder. The only other person who knew about it was Brian Hadaway and his involvement in the case was finished, so he could just disappear into the sunset to count his money. He had made Price swear to keep it a secret as it would have been so humiliating for Barlocks he might have had to resign. Yet here was Price spilling the beans already. Price said the evidence was ridiculous and would have got laughed out of court. But once he had discovered there wasn't a murder, he quickly hushed it up and went back to Manchester even trying to claim some credit for solving the mystery. He explained that Spiffington-Smythe had transformed from a right-wing hate filled fanatic into a born-again Christian. He claimed it was the death of his mother, a devout Catholic that triggered a reaction in him and changed his entire outlook on the world. He went to live with some monks on a monastery in the Outer Hebrides. He had come out of hiding when word had got to him that his body had supposedly been discovered. The Abbot at the monastery had tried to keep him from finding out about it, but just like everywhere else news gets around. It seems there are gossips even in a place where there isn't much talking, and in a place where newspapers, internet, and telephones aren't allowed.

Spiffington-Smythe had announced that he had no intention of returning to the monastery. He had been given a mission from God and had unfinished business in politics. He intended creating a new political party and would try to get elected again. He had every chance of succeeding. His army of foreigner hating followers had grown significantly during his hiatus from society. Barney cringed at the thought of his return, but at the same time was relieved that he had come back. Even thought it was unlikely he would have been found guilty of murder, there would always be people who would question his innocence. The people Barney referred to as the 'no smoke without fire brigade'.

The identity of the person buried in the garden was never solved. There was very little useful evidence to go on. The bracelet was similar to the one Spiffington-Smythe wore, but it was impossible to tell who this one belonged to. Price chose not to mention the involvement of Alison's former husband in the case. Kenneth was safely back in prison and Price didn't see any value in making his involvement known.

After dinner he received a call from Alison. She had been released with a caution and was back at home. The police hadn't charged anyone with anything. They had accepted Alison was severely provoked, and Sue hadn't been too badly hurt. Alison had been lucky, but perhaps not as lucky as Fiona who wasn't charged for her violent chair throwing incident. She also was given a caution. Barney said his goodbyes, put Jack and Louis in the car and set off. On the journey home he spoke to Jack.

'Jack, I have something important to tell you.'

'What is it, Daddy?'

'Were you listening when I was telling Grandma about something that happened to Mummy last night?'

'No.'

'Are you sure?'

'Yes.'

'That's good. Because Mummy was arrested by the police for getting drunk and punching someone in the face in the pub. And that's not something I want you to know about.'

'Alright Daddy.'

'When you go to school on Monday, don't forget you mustn't tell everybody, especially Mrs Solly that your mum was arrested by the police for getting drunk and punching someone in the face in the pub on Friday. Don't forget now. Don't let daddy down. I'm relying on you.'

37

A week had passed since the events at the Oddfellows Arms. Life had returned to normal. Well, almost normal. Alison was not in a good mood and most of her anger was aimed at Barney. He felt this was most unfair. It's her precious son who in her eyes can do no wrong who she should be airing her grievances to. It must have been Jack who told all of the class at school about Alison's arrest. How could she blame Barney? He had told Jack specifically not to mention it. What made her even more peeved was that when Mrs Solly phoned and asked one of them to go and collect Jack, Barney had made some weak excuse to get out of it and Alison had to go. It was an embarrassing experience for her, and she wondered how Jack had found out about it. She had one theory involving her devious husband but couldn't prove it. No doubt Jack would grass him up as usual, but he would enjoy it while it lasted.

'Are just planning on sitting in front of the television all day?'

'Yes. Pretty much.'

'There're a few jobs need doing.'

'I can't help. I've got to take the dog for a walk.'

'We don't have a dog.'

'Oh yeah. I forgot. But you know my motto. Why do today something you can put off until tomorrow?'

Before it could develop into an argument they were interrupted by the sound of Action by Def Leppard, the ring tone on Barney's phone. The display said Mum. He tutted loudly.

'What does she want now? I only saw her a week ago. It'll be a squeaky door or a drippy tap. Why doesn't she get her new fiancé to fix it. On second thoughts that's not such a good idea. I wouldn't trust him anywhere near a spanner or a can of WD-40.'

He answered the phone.

'Hello Mum.'

'Hello Cecil. I'm afraid I'm calling you with some bad news. Your dad has had a heart attack. I'm not sure how serious it is yet, but he's been taken to Wexham Park Hospital. It's near Slough.'

'I know where it is. That's where Alison was taken when she had her heart attack. Also, I used to go there to repair their vending machines for many years.'

'That's alright then. You should be able to find it alright. I assume you're going to go? You're all he's got really.'

'Yes. Of course I'll go. Let me know if you hear any more meanwhile.'

Barney explained it all to Alison, then packed a bag and set off yet again on the long journey south. His dad wasn't the sort to get ill. He was never ill. But time eventually takes its toll on everyone, and he was 77 years old. His dad hated hospitals. He felt sorry for the doctors and nurses who would have to care for him.

It was a slow and boring journey, partly his own fault because he was still too mean to pay for the M6 toll road. He called at his dad's house in Maidenhead to collect some bits and pieces that he thought might come in useful. Then he continued his journey to Slough and arrived at the hospital in late afternoon. By now he was very tired. He wandered around several corridors looking for the ward his dad was in, passing a selection of vending machines he used to be responsible for back in the day. He chuckled as he saw an out of order sign on one of them. Then he thought he saw one of his old work colleagues Colin walking towards the broken machine. Colin was the most boring man in the world, and the last person he wanted to bump into. He wasn't sure it was him, but he suddenly switched direction to avoid being spotted.

He never found out whether it was this distraction, or his tiredness, or a loose floor tile. He tripped and stumbled forward. He instinctively threw out his hands, but it failed to work. His head crashed onto the ground, and everything went black.

He must have been unconscious for several hours. He woke up in a hospital bed with a painful head and arm, and there were bandages everywhere. He heard someone laughing.

'Thanks for coming to visit me son. I hope you had a nice trip. Oops sorry.'

'You're welcome. But go easy on the laughing. I'm in a lot of pain here.'

'You silly sod. Only you could come to visit me in hospital and I end up visiting you instead.'

He continued to laugh until a nurse intervened.

'Mr Barnard. You must get back to bed at once. You are in no condition to be walking around.'

'Stop making a fuss. There's nothing wrong with me.'

'I'll be the judge of that. Now return to your bed. Please.'

Barney could hear the sound of his dad laughing fade into the distance and he fell back into unconsciousness. He woke up the following morning and a nurse gave him a report of his injuries. Although he didn't understand all the gobbledegook, it didn't sound too bad. He lay there for another two hours getting bored. Then another member of staff came up to his bedside.

'Mr Barnard. I'm afraid I've got some bad news for you.'

Barney didn't like the sound of that and went into a panic.

'What? But… but your nurse just told me it wasn't anything serious. Just a bit of concussion and a few cuts and bruises.'

'No, not you. You'll be fine. It's your father. I'm afraid he passed away during the night.'

38

The next few days were difficult for him to put it mildly. Firstly, he had to recover from his own accident. He now had a pair of black eyes. The damage from the darts punch up still hadn't completely faded away and now he had another eye to match. Meanwhile he had to deal with the loss of his dad. He had to spend one more night in hospital and then he went back to his dad's house. He had a lot of stuff to sort through. But he ended up just doing nothing and sat around the house for two days before deciding to drive home. He could return with Alison and maybe even his mum. They could go through all of his stuff together and decide what to keep, what to take to the charity shop, and what to throw away.

It was a long and lonely drive home. His emotions were all over the place. His dad had been fit and healthy. This had come from nothing. It felt so unfair. On the other hand, some would say that's the way to go. You wouldn't want to live through a long and undignified illness waiting for death would you? People have differing views, but Barney decided he would rather go quickly just like his dad had. He also gained some comfort knowing his dad had spent his final few hours laughing his head off. That was definitely a good way to go. And then he felt angry because he was the one that was being laughed at.

On arrival home Alison gave him a hug, then held him for a long time without saying anything while his emotions came flooding out. It wasn't the first time she'd seen him in tears. He didn't see anything wrong with having a good cry now and again. If it was alright for women and little children to cry, then why isn't it acceptable for a middle-aged man? There were so many horrible things going on in the world. People starving. Disease. Refugees. Unnecessary wars. Oppression. Discrimination. All kinds of cruelty. Last week he had been watching a news report where a man had been beaten to death in front of his seven-year-old g'daughter by a gang of thugs while waiting for a bus. He felt that anyone who could watch that and not be reduced to tears must have something seriously wrong with them. This time it was slightly different. It wasn't the problems of society that had upset him. It was the loss of his dad. But the crying had done him good. He suddenly felt a lot better.

Alison sensed it and finally broke the silence and decided a spot of humour would be the kindest approach.

'Did you enjoy your trip?'

'Yes. Dad has already tried that one on me before laughing himself to death at his own joke. And how have you been? Have you punched anyone in my absence?'

'No. My hooligan days are over. But I don't regret what I did. That woman had it coming. Talking of which, are you finally going to own up and tell me how Jack found out about what happened?'

'I can't imagine. But it wasn't anything to do with me.'

A little figure appeared through the door.

'Yes it was. Daddy told me all about it.'

39

The next morning Alison was awake first. She watched Barney as he went through his usual slow routine of waking up. He talked in his sleep quite often, especially when he was about to wake up. She sometimes found it irritating, but this morning she found it funny. He finally awoke from a pleasant dream about a woman who he thought might have been Kylie Minogue. Alison spoke first and brought him back to reality.

'How are you feeling this morning?'

'I'm feeling a bit stiff.'

'I didn't mean physically. I meant your state of mind after the trauma of yesterday.'

'Not too bad. I'm used to Jack grassing me up.'

'Not that, you dummy. I'm talking about your dad.'

'Yeah, I know. I'm ok. I kind of view death like the Klingons in Star Trek do. They look upon death not as something to mourn, but rather a celebration of their life. Obviously, it doesn't work that way if it was someone who had died young, especially a child, or someone who had died in tragic circumstances, but my dad had a decent long life, or perhaps I should say he had a good innings as he was such a big cricket fan, so now that I'm over the initial shock I'm not going to be down about it.'

'I know what you mean. I am in an unusual situation in that the death of my parents was the most positive moment in my life. Losing them inspired me to take action and leave Kenneth and my horrible marriage. They died for a noble cause. I must be a Klingon too.'

They lay there quietly for a few moments before Alison changed the subject.

'How can you be feeling stiff? It's not as if you did a two-hour session in the gym yesterday or went for a five mile run.'

Barney rolled over onto his side and pressed up against her.

'I don't mean that sort of stiff. I mean this sort of stiff.'

'You can just put that thing back in its box. I have to get up and go to the school with Jack. Then I've also got a showdown with Mrs Solly.'

'Thanks a lot. Now the mental image of Mrs Solly is going to put me off.'

'Good. I told you I haven't got time this morning.'

'It's still early. You don't have to go just yet. We've got time for a quickie.'

'I've told you a thousand times, I don't do quickies.'

'Come on. It's your duty.'

'My duty? What century have we gone back to? A man no longer owns his wife. They don't say love honour and obey any longer in wedding vows.'

'No, you misunderstand. I meant it's your moral duty.'

'My moral duty?'

'Yes. Because you caused the situation, it is only right that you help with the solution.'

'What on earth are you on about?'

'You're lying there all warm and naked and sexy and…'

'If I could just stop you right there. Fake flattery will get you nowhere.'

'It's not fake.'

'Yes it is. You were dreaming about Kylie Minogue. It was her that put the lead in your pencil.'

'What? But… How could… That's… That's creepy. What makes you say that? How did you know?'

'You said her name as you were waking up. Oh Kylie.'

'It's a bit much when a man can't even have a bit of privacy in his own dreams now.'

'Then try not to reveal them out loud.'

'Whether it was Kylie or you that was the cause, it doesn't change anything. Kylie isn't here, so I'll have to make do with you.'

'You silver tongued devil you. How can a girl say no to that?'

'But you still are saying no.'

'Look. I'll only be gone for an hour or so. Then I'll be back before you know it.'

'By then I will be shrivelled up like a slug that has had salt sprinkled on it.'

'I know a few tricks to revive a dead slug.'

'Really? Sounds interesting. Such as?'

Alison burst into song.

'I should be so lucky. Lucky, lucky, lucky. I should be so lucky…'

'If I could just stop you there. I've got a better idea. Let's both go to the school and team up against Mrs Solly. It's about time we started making a few demands. This is our son's future at stake. We need to start fighting for him.'

'Yes, you're right. Let's do it. Then afterwards you can take me to the pub you're always on about. The one with the chicken wings. Have a couple of drinks.'

'Okay. You're on.'

'Then we can come back here and check out the salty slug situation.'

'It's a date. And for your information pencils don't contain lead. They are made with graphite, a non-toxic form of carbon that is mixed with clay at various ratios depending on how hard you want the pencil.'

'Shut up.'

Epilogue

Fifteen Years Later

'Oh god, that's disgusting. Open the window. It must be all that gassy lager you were drinking.'

'Don't look at me. I think your mate in the back might have had something to do with it. He's not stopped eating all day. If anything's gassy around here it's him.'

'But he's asleep.'

'Being asleep doesn't stop you farting, just ask your mum. Although I must admit that's an impressive effort managing to knock out one as bad as that in your sleep.'

Louis stirred from his sleep.

'Urrgh! Who was that?'

'Our money is on you.'

'Oh. You could be right. I feel another one is on its way.'

Barney and jack frantically opened their windows in anticipation. Just in the nick of time. Louis repeated the trick, only this time very loudly. The mood in the car wasn't great. Sunderland hadn't been expected to win. Now that Slough Town were owned by China and had a vast fortune at their disposal, they were storming up the various leagues and were hopeful of being in the premiership within the next two years. But even so, they would have liked to see them put up a bit more of a fight. To lose 2-3 at home to anyone isn't good enough. To make matters even worse Sunderland had what appeared to be a perfectly good goal disallowed for a foul. Jack was particularly angry about it.

'That referee was a disgrace. That was never a foul. If it wasn't for him, we would have got a draw.'

'That is not necessarily true.'

'Of course it's true. Did you not do maths in school in your days? It ended up 2-3. If that goal had stood it would have been 3-3. It's simple enough.'

'It isn't that simple. If the referee had allowed that goal the game would have restarted with a kick off from the centre spot instead of a free kick near their goal. So a completely different game would have taken place form the one that actually did. We might have got the draw as you say. Or we might even have won. Or we might have lost 3-6 or something.'

'Rubbish.'

Louis chipped in from the back seat.

'No it's not. I've got to agree with your dad on this one. He's got a point.'

Barney was impressed. The least intelligent person in the car understood what he meant.

Jack was driving again. Barney wanted to drive, but Jack insisted, because Barney had drunk four pints before the match. Barney wasn't happy about that but knew that Jack would go running to his mum and tell her he was driving over the limit. He decided it wasn't worth the earache he would get from her.

'If you insist on driving, can't you go a bit faster? We won't be home until midnight at this rate.'

'There's a thing called the speed limit in this country. I know you don't take any notice of it. That's why you've got points on your licence while there's none on mine. That's why you've done umpteen speed awareness courses, and I haven't done any. You old people drive far too dangerously.'

'I am not an old people. I am middle aged. And I haven't caused any accidents and I've been driving for over forty years.'

'I don't know why we couldn't have just booked into some posh hotel in Sunderland and travelled back tomorrow. Louis and I could have had a night on the town. You and Neil could have gone somewhere dull for another game of darts.'

'Sunderland doesn't have any posh hotels.'

'So where does the king stay when he visits?'

'He's got a caravan at South Shields. Anyway, hotels are expensive, and as I told you on the way up, I'm not made of money.'

'And as I told you on the way up, yes you are. Mum always said you were a skinflint.'

'Mum said, mum said, mum said. I don't know why you don't just go shopping for shoes with her instead of coming to the football.'

'I've heard there's a nice hotel in Seaham. It's really plush and has a spa. When Sunderland were owned by that millionaire American businessman, he used to stay there. If it's good enough for him, it's good enough for us. We could have checked in for the night. Then had a night out in Seaham Harbour. Rumour has it all the girls go out in miniskirts and skimpy tops, even on bitterly cold nights in January.'

'I'm a bit old to be chasing after girls in miniskirts and skimpy tops. Besides, what would your mum say? No doubt you would tell her I was looking at girls.'

'I didn't mean for you to come. Just Louis and I.'

'Great. And what am I supposed to do then while you two are running around in miniskirts and skimpy tops?'

They continued in silence for another ten minutes. Then Jack spoke again.

'Another advantage of staying in a hotel would be that we might not get back in time to go to Grandma's house tomorrow. I assume we're going to Grandma's house tomorrow?'

'Yes we are. We go every Sunday.'

'Can't you come up with one of your lame excuses and get us out of it?'

'Just tell her you are staying at home to do something more enjoyable.'

'What, you mean such as sticking pins in your eyeballs?'

Jack and Barney laughed, but Louis didn't see the funny side.'

'You are a pair of ungrateful bastards. I wish I still had a grandmother who would cook me a roast dinner every Sunday. My grandma died when I was ten years old, and my nan only died last year.'

'Sorry Louis. That was a bit tactless of me. I wasn't thinking. It's not as bad as we are making out. She is a very good cook. Besides, there's no way Jack wouldn't go. Mumsy and

Grandma are not going to be let down by their darling little baby boy.'

'Yawn. Think of a new one. I'm surprised you even get invited to Grandma's after virtually ruining their wedding.'

'What are you on about? I didn't ruin their wedding.'

'You made a few inappropriate comments about their religion. That wasn't the time or place to do that.'

'It was hard not to. The whole thing was a tribute to God and Jesus. I half expected the big cheese himself to pop down from heaven and be the special guest.'

'I know. But did you really need to tell them that?'

'Some people can't take a joke.'

'If it turns out you're wrong and there really is a heaven and hell, I know which way you'll be heading.'

'Not necessarily. What if God doesn't have much time for the people who believe in him? He's supposed to be wise. I bet he thinks anyone who believes in him must be a nutcase.'

'There's only one nutcase around here.'

'Why? Because I don't blindly accept what I'm told? I think God will gladly welcome me into heaven, or should I say his bouncer St Peter will. I would imagine he will be glad of a bit of company from someone sane for a change. And the likes of you will burn in hell for eternity.'

'I don't think so. I will be let in too. I'm an atheist too. If I apply your logic, God will want me up there too. Whereas you won't last long in heaven. You'll just go around causing trouble and incur His wrath. Then you'll be banished. Just like you were from many of your vending customers premises.'

'That could work out for the best. Going to hell might not be such a bad thing. I would just get bored spending eternity sitting on a cloud getting fed grapes by an angel. And the music is going to be terrible. Probably Cliff Richard or Aled Jones. All the best bands will be in hell. It would be like one big never ending rock festival. And all the flames will make for a spectacular backdrop.'

They continued the rest of the journey in silence. Jack insisted on listening to Radio Z, which as the driver he had the right to choose. Can't Get You Out of My Head by Kylie Minogue came on. Jack took the opportunity to be mischievous.

'Kylie Minogue? Isn't she the one you have fantasies about?'

'What are you talking about?'

'Someone told me you were having a dream about her and shouted out her name in your sleep.'

'And we all know who that someone is, don't we? Mummy, mummy, mummy.'

'Is it true then? Were you having an erotic dream about Kylie Minogue?'

'Why should it be erotic? I might have shouted her name because she was trying to murder me or something.'

Louis decided to chip in with some words of wisdom.

'Look on the bright side. At least Kylie Minogue is a good-looking bird. Think yourself lucky it wasn't Margaret Thatcher or Theresa May or somebody.'

'Yes. That would have been some nightmare. What is someone

of your age doing referring to women as birds anyway? I would have thought your generation was a bit more enlightened. It would seem the human race is taking an awfully long time to evolve.'

'Most of the chicks I know don't mind being called birds.'

'Why does that not surprise me?'

Barney was suffering from his own rules. He didn't like the music they played, and he thought the presenters were annoying berks who liked the sound of their own voices. They were having some kind of phone in where they were asking anyone whose birthday it was tomorrow to call in and tell them if they were doing anything special for their birthday. A string of boring or dumb people obliged and the presenter did his best to have a laugh at their expense. A woman named Sophie phoned in.

'Hello Sophie. I understand it's your birthday tomorrow?'

'Yes it is John.'

'And are you doing anything special?'

'Yes. My husband is taking me up the Shard.'

Jack and Louis sniggered like naughty schoolboys. Barney didn't. But he sensed that the presenter was going to have some fun with this woman.

'Oh, that should be nice. Has he ever taken you up the Shard before?'

Jack and Louis were now laughing out loud.

'No, this will be my first time.'

'Have you ever been taken up the Shard by anyone else?'

'No.'

'Well I hope you enjoy it. It was nice talking to you Sophie. Goodbye.'

The presenter ended the call. By now Jack and Louis were laughing hysterically. Barney wasn't impressed.

'You're going to crash the car in a minute if you don't calm down. Is that what passes as humour these days? Smutty innuendo? Some plonker making a gullible person look even more stupid?'

'These days? I was watching a documentary last week about comedy on television in the 70s and 80s. Smutty innuendo was all they had. Except for racism, sexism, and homophobia. But no doubt you'll tell me that they don't make comedy like they used to. I've seen all the rants on social media. You aren't allowed to say anything these days. The woke lefties and the politically correct brigade have ruined comedy. People are too easily offended etc. etc. blah blah blah blah.'

'You don't really know me all that well, do you? I hated that sort of so-called comedy too. I just don't think a joke about being taken up the Shard warrants the sort of hysteria it induced in you two.'

They were almost home. Jack said, 'Would it be ok if Louis and I get out at the pub, and you take the car home?'

'I see. You've come down from your moral high horse? You said I'd had too many drinks to drive. Or does that only apply when it suits you?'

'Enough time has passed. You should be ok now.'

'Go on then. I'll be glad to see the back of you. And take your friend and his smelly Shard with you. I'm going to have to get the car fumigated.'

Jack and Louis got out and went into the pub. As soon as they were out of sight he started laughing. He laughed all the way back home.

Available worldwide from Amazon

---

www.mtp.agency

www.facebook.com/mtp.agency

@mtp_agency

Michael Terence Publishing

Printed in Great Britain
by Amazon

50533424R00126